COMING HOME

AVA GRAY

ALSO BY AVA GRAY

CONTEMPORARY ROMANCE

Playing with Trouble Series:

Chasing What's Mine

Claiming What's Mine

Protecting What's Mine

Saving What's Mine

Alpha Billionaire Series

Secret Baby with Brother's Best Friend

Just Pretending

Loving The One I Should Hate

Billionaire and the Barista

Coming Home

Doctor Daddy

Standalone's:

Ruthless Love

The Best Friend Affair

PARANORMAL ROMANCE

Maple Lake Shifters Series:

Omega Vanished

Omega Exiled

Omega Coveted

Everton Falls Mated Love Series:

The Alpha's Mate

The Wolf's Wild Mate

Saving His Mate

Fighting For His Mate

Dragons of Las Vegas Series:

Thin Ice

Silver Lining

A Spark in the Dark

Fire & Ice

Dragons of Las Vegas Boxed Set (The Complete Series)

Standalone's:

Fiery Kiss

Wild Fate

BLURB

I found out that I was pregnant with his baby...

Then I found out that he was leaving me.

The thought of it was unbearable.

Holden was my brother's best friend.

Being with him was forbidden, and oh-so-wrong.

My brother would have *not* been happy to say the least.

But that didn't stop me from falling into bed with him.

Or from giving him my heart.

I spent sleepless nights thinking about him.

Finding out that I was pregnant shocked me.

But it was nothing compared to what I had to do after.

I couldn't tell Holden about it.

I had to let him follow his dream.

More than anything, I had to protect him from my brother.

But all hell would break loose once he found out what I'd kept hidden from him: A little girl that has her father's eyes.

Would he ever come home to meet her?

1

MAKENZIE

Present...

I stood in the back with my parents and brother. We arrived a few minutes late, not surprising as we never seemed to be on time for anything as a family, even now that we were all adults. I twisted my fingers and continuously rubbed my hands together.

My feet were killing me. I couldn't remember why I had picked the shoes I was wearing. Maybe it had something to do with wanting to dress appropriately, maybe I wanted to look cute?

What was wrong with me?

Why was I dressing cute for a funeral?

It was the first time in several years that I would see Holden, and I put on heels slightly higher than was socially acceptable for the occasion. Thinking had not been involved. Holden would be distracted with his mother, and his own emotions. He certainly wouldn't be looking at my outfit, or thinking I was cute. But I hadn't thought of any of that when I got dressed. All I could focus on was Holden coming home, and that I was going to see him again.

And now that we were at the funeral, I saw him. He looked grim. Of course, he would, we were all there to bury his father, Powell Wells.

I had basically grown up knowing Mr. Wells. He was a friend of my parents, and as a kid every summer I was running in and out of the Well's beach house nearly as much as Holden was running in and out of my family's house. I wasn't one of those kids who adopted my friend's parents, and honestly, I really wasn't much of Holden's friend. But I still remembered the man as being a constant adult in my life, especially during the summers.

Holden was my brother's best friend, and I was the little sister running after them for someone to play with and grab a little bit of attention.

I don't know if Travis and Holden met because our parents knew each other, or they met because we summered on Nantucket at the same time, or had they met at boarding school. They met, and they were inseparable. Not only did they go to the same boarding schools, insisting on attending the same high school, they even went to NYU together and roomed together.

I was in the way, always in the way.

Travis leaned into me. "Will you stop fidgeting," he growled.

Mom patted him on the back of his hand. I wasn't sure if that was to soothe him or quiet him.

"My feet hurt," I whispered.

She rested her hand over mine. Her touch was definitely an attempt to soothe me, to calm me down.

"You shouldn't have worn those ridiculous shoes. Who wears six-inch pumps to a grave-side service?"

"I thought we would be sitting."

Mom tightened her grip on the back of my hand. That was to get me to shut up. I put my other hand on top of hers and squeezed back signalling that I got the message loud and clear, sorry, I will do better. At least that was my intention.

Mr. Wells had been a popular man, rich, and well regarded. He owned and ran several companies that did something with airplanes. I had always been impressed that he flew his family to the island from Connecticut in his very own airplane. We always took the ferry over.

I tried to decide how many people at the funeral were employees. I guess the rough looking bunch of men toward the back all were. They were dressed solemnly, but the clothes were not necessarily black, and certainly were not designer labels.

I continued my game with who was there because they actually liked him, or because he had been an important business contact. The front row was family and friends, other people I recognized from my child-hood. That's where we should have been had we arrived on time.

The rows after that were filled with old men who looked red-faced and uncomfortable in their expensive suits and ties. I figured them to be the bankers and the lawyers. Those people were here because Powell Wells had made them a lot of money over the years, and it was only polite to send off a client like that. I let my mind play guessing games as I looked at the expensively dressed women. Were any of them his mistress? I decided that if Mr. Wells had kept a side chick, she wasn't here.

By that point in the funeral, I had fidgeted and made up stories about everyone in attendance. I was going to have to suck it up and do the one thing I had managed to not do, look at Holden.

I had let my gaze identify him long enough to know where he was seated so that I could avoid looking at him. I was afraid if I started looking at him, I wouldn't be able to stop. And if he looked at me, I would embarrass myself and do something horrifically stupid and embarrass everyone else in attendance. No one wanted that, especially me.

I was really afraid that if I looked at him, he might look back at me. I didn't know what I would do if that happened. I considered that dropping dead of pure mortification was a possibility.

I twisted to see if there were more interesting people for me to look at, make up stories about. I caught a glimpse of my father. He sniffled and his eyes were rimmed in red. I felt like a selfish fool. Looping my hand through Dad's arm, I rested my head on his shoulder.

The reason Mr. Wells had been a constant in my youth was because he was my father's friend. And here I was making up stories about the people attending the man's funeral while my dad was mourning the loss of a friend. I didn't think Holden's parents were any older than mine. I closed my eyes against the thought of losing either mom or dad.

Holden must be hurting. Was anyone up there holding his hand, offering him support, or was he being a solid rock of support for his mother?

It didn't take bravery to open my eyes and search out Holden. It had been cowardice to not look at him before. I sucked in a small gasp when I let my gaze rest on him. He looked as if he had been beaten, physically and mentally.

Of course, I had heard there had been an accident. His mom told my mom, she passed it along to both Travis and me. It was the only way we got any news about Holden; the direct lines of communication had been severed several years earlier. Having known about an accident hadn't prepared me for what that meant.

His mother rested her head on his shoulder. He had his good arm around her, his other arm was wrapped in thick white bandages and supported in a dark sling. His left leg, the same side as the broken arm, was also wrapped in bandages and propped in front of him.

The bandaged limbs had a weird impact on my perception of him in his dress uniform. He should have been tall and strong, and irresistible. Instead, he seemed small. He had bruises on his face, and black eye, a strip of tape across the bridge of his nose. His expression was dour. Was it from the pain he had to be in from the injuries, or from his father's death? Was it both?

There sat a man who I remembered as being larger than life, full of vitality, strength, and power, and he was anything but that. He'd gotten into a fight with life's challenges and clearly had not won. What had happened to him? Had his helicopter gone down? All I knew was 'accident,' but no details.

Holden didn't need me staring at him during one of the most difficult times of his life. He wasn't on display for my visual consumption.

Just as I realised I needed to stop staring, he looked up at me. Our eyes met. I should have looked at him earlier. I couldn't reach out and offer comfort, but I sensed him drawing comfort and strength from my gaze. It wasn't until that point that I started crying. Tears leaked out of the corners of my eyes as I felt Holden's sadness.

The officiant ended the service, and people stood. My eye contact with Holden was broken. Whatever connection we had formed was severed in that moment.

Mom grabbed my elbow. "We should go give Millie and Holden our condolences."

I couldn't move. My feet, in their ridiculous shoes, would not budge. Panic knotted in my stomach. I couldn't handle their grief anymore; I had already given Holden everything I could. I would break down if I went up there.

"I can't," I managed to say.

"Come on Makenzie, the Wells family are very close friends, you should—" Dad started before Travis cut him off.

"It's okay. I get it. Stay here, I'll give Holden your condolences. She's sad, let her be."

Dad nodded in agreement, and they walked up to the family. I couldn't see faces, too many people were in the way. But I did make eye contact one last time with Holden before we left. For a second, I understood I had made the wrong decision, but then he closed his eyes, and I knew I was forgiven.

2

HOLDEN

I f there was ever a time to say, 'fuck my life,' today would be that day.

It had only been a few days since I got a call that I hadn't expected to get for years. My father was dead, come home immediately. Being in the military wasn't an issue, they would grant me bereavement leave. The problem was that I was strung out on painkillers less than two weeks after a major surgery and a life-changing accident.

Mom had already been through enough. First me, and then dad.

That night after the call, in my painkiller fogged-up brain, my dreams went sideways. Instead of me in the wreckage, it was dad. Instead of screaming metal and burning buildings, dad was screaming, dad was collapsing. Of course, at that time I hadn't yet learned that dad suffered a massive brain aneurysm and died at his desk. That might have made my nightmares worse.

I really wasn't in any condition to travel, still suffering the lingering effects of surgery to both my left leg and arm, two broken ribs, and a severe concussion. But there wasn't any way to not be there.

The next few days at home were surreal with my aunts bustling about taking care of everything, including me.

"Are you comfortable?" one of them asked. She arranged the pillows under my propped-up leg and made sure my arm was also well supported. She adjusted the volume on the TV they had brought into the large sitting room so that I could have something to entertain me, and I could be in a location where they could more easily keep an eye on me.

I squinted and tried to remember her name. The painkillers had my brain looping out on weird thoughts. "How did you get out of the TV?"

"Holden, you are saying the craziest things on those pain pills. I really should remember to record you. I'll bring you some water. You rest."

"Okay," I mumbled.

The next time my aunt walked by, she was in something different, and it took an effort to remind myself that I had identical twins for aunts. They were Dad's younger twin sisters. Random memories came back and suddenly I was a child and having things explained how it was perfect for there to be two girls, one each to be named after the grandmothers.

I was an only son, continuing another family tradition of being named after my grandfather, Holden Wells. If I ever had a son, I would continue the tradition and name him for my father, Powell.

Mom stayed in bed the entire time until the local priest arrived.

I didn't remember Mom being a regular Sunday morning churchgoer, but maybe that had changed since I left. Or maybe she had the entire time and I had never paid enough attention.

Father Jones seemed to offer her comfort that no one else had been able to provide. He was a soft-spoken man, and as he went over the readings, Olivia and Lydia sat on either side of mom, holding her hands, literally propping her up.

I was too deep in pain pills to be much good to anybody. But I needed to be there.

Dad had been entirely too young; aneurysms didn't discriminate for age.

I vaguely remembered speaking to a lawyer regarding the will. One of my aunts— I think it was Lydia. It might have been Olivia— intervened on my behalf, reminding the lawyer that I was on painkillers and not a responsible party.

He blustered and bellowed, "Who is a responsible party around here?"

At that point, the aunt showed him the door and told him to learn some manners.

Not that those whirlwind days after arriving home were entertaining or enjoyable, but I would have given anything to go back to them instead of sitting at this uncomfortable funeral. Those few days had been too busy to feel grief, too unregulated on my meds to feel much of anything.

The morning of the funeral, I sucked it up and cut my dosage in half. I needed to be present, in all of my pain today. I needed to be coherent enough to provide the comfort and support my mother deserved. Getting ready had been a challenge, even with assistance. I was ever so grateful for my aunts and their organizational skills. A liveried driver arrived for us and had a wheelchair for me. He must have been a specially trained driver because he assisted me in and out of the car.

Mom held it together until we arrived at the private viewing.

I kept the wheelchair back and allowed her last private moments together with Dad. From where I sat, Dad simply looked to be asleep. I wished I could be of more support, physically, when Lydia collapsed in on herself in her grief. I couldn't get up and go to her, providing a steady shoulder. She had been so steadfast in the days prior.

I wheeled up next to Mom and took her hand. Life was going to be very different with Dad gone.

"It's time for us to go," Olivia came up and spoke.

I turned and saw one of the funeral servicemen standing behind her. He must have come in and found the one person who looked like they were holding it together the best to have let the rest of us know it was time to say our last goodbyes.

"No, I don't want to, not just yet" Mom managed. Her voice was so small, so sad.

"People will already be arriving at the cemetery."

"Let them," I said. "We can be a little late. Give her some more time."

I wanted more time too. I wanted to ask him all those things I thought we would have time for later. Questions about his life, my life, and all the things I didn't know I would have to navigate for a long time yet but were now my responsibility. I needed to know where he kept the important legal documents, what did his life insurance policy cover, how did I make sure the right properties were in Mom's name, and how much was in my name? There was more the lawyer had thrown at me in my pain-killer haze. I would have to call and find out what to do next.

Mom finally nodded and we left. The funeral home waited until we left before they closed the lid on Dad's coffin.

There was a crowd at the cemetery waiting for our arrival, not that we were more than a few minutes late. Our driver transferred me from the car into the wheelchair and rolled me into position. Mom sat by my side; my hand clasped in her vice-like grip.

Pain distorted my perception of time nearly as much as the pain-killer meds had. Maybe cutting my dose hadn't been the best idea, but I had wanted to be mentally present and not wonder if the priest's bushy eyebrows could talk— something I had thought about when he visited the house.

In an attempt to occupy my brain, distract it from the pain in my body and in my heart, I let my gaze drift over the people in attendance. I expected to see the Underwood family sitting in the first few rows. It hurt that they hadn't come. I didn't expect the entire family, but not seeing the parents was a bit of a blow. My eyes kept moving over the crowd until I saw them. The entire family.

My gaze passed over their son and landed on their daughter, Makenzie. I hadn't seen her for years. My heart clenched at how incredibly beautiful she looked. Her eyes were closed, and she rested against her father. They must have gotten there even later than we had for them to be standing in the back.

When she opened her eyes and our gazes locked, I felt hope for the first time since before things had literally fallen down around me. Anticipation built in my belly when the service ended, and I expected the Underwood family to pay their condolences. I would get to see Makenzie again, hear her voice.

"You look like you dealt a shit blow."

I looked up to the sarcastic tones of Travis Underwood.

I gave him a curt nod. I could hear his mother cooing to mine regarding loss and grief and sorrow. I was stuck with an asshole being an asshole.

"Sorry about your loss man," Travis actually said something nice.

I looked past his mother to see if Makenzie was in line, but she wasn't. Couldn't she even talk to me today of all the days?

"Makenzie was too torn up to come over, but she did want me to give you, her condolences."

I reached up to shake his hand.

He took it and gave me a power squeeze, yeah man, I get it you're strong and I'm broken. Travis leaned in and through gritted teeth hissed, "Never talk to or look at my sister again. Do you hear me?"

I leveled a glare at him. "Loud and clear."

3

MAKENZIE

Seven years earlier...

"Mom, I'm headed out to the beach!" My brother had no manners.

Two years away at college and he'd turn feral. Mom had raised us to not yell like that. I was in my room getting ready and I could hear him. Then again, the summer house on Nantucket was a lot older with thinner walls than the home in Upstate New York was.

When he slammed the door the walls in my bedroom shook. That explained why I heard him so well, my bedroom was directly above the back door. I didn't hear mom as she walked with her perfectly clipped steps, and I didn't hear her open the door, but I certainly heard her yell.

"Travis Underwood, where do you think you are that you can yell into the house like that and then slam a door? Get back here and speak to me properly."

"Mom!"

I threw open my window and leaned out. This was going to be entertaining. I didn't care if Travis saw me or not.

Mom cleared her throat.

Travis made an elaborate shrug, dropping the cooler he was carrying, and rolling his eyes before walking back. It didn't matter how old he was, Mom wasn't going to put up with him for not behaving. Maybe she should have sent him to Europe for one summer instead of me.

My parents actually sent me to finish school. Mom had wanted me to go before I embarked on my collegiate life, not that freshman year at Mary Brooks had been terribly different from my senior year at Lady Mont Academy. The same type of girl, different classes, not uniform, but the rest hadn't seemed like a change at all.

I attended what was essentially a hostess training boot camp for rich girls at what felt like a Swiss monastery. I could put on a mean cocktail party, making sure I curated my guest list for the most interesting of conversations.

My brother got to hang out in New York City and act like a bro-dude, and bum around at the beach. I wanted to go to the beach. And after a year of missing it, I really wanted to lay out in the sun and not think about napkin placement.

"Mother," he grumbled. "I am going to be late. I'm picking Holden up and we're headed to the beach."

"Why aren't you taking your sister?"

"She isn't invited." He was twenty-one and he still hated to have me tag along.

Not that I wanted to hang out with him and his stupid friend. Sure, I chased after them plenty over the years to get them to play with me. But I learned, chasing after friends to play with you meant they weren't your friends. At about the same time I realized boys were, for lack of a better word, icky. I had to have been eleven or twelve when I stopped wanting my brother to be my friend. That's probably the summer I started sewing. Fabric and patterns became my friends.

They still were. But that didn't mean I wouldn't bug Travis to at least give me a ride down to the beach with him. I closed my window and finished pulling on a cover-up. I shoved my feet into flip-flops and grabbed my bag.

I was downstairs and hovering behind Mom before she was done giving him a piece of her mind.

"Oh, look, Makenzie is all ready," she said.

He glared at me.

"I won't talk to you, I won't bother you for a drink, I won't even be near you, and I'll walk home. Please?" I begged.

"Sit in the back. Don't even say hi to Holden."

"Why would I?" Holden was as big of an obnoxious bro-dude as my brother, more so. Holden was boring, and not particularly attractive. It was a good thing he came from a very rich family, otherwise why would any of the girls be interested in him?

I kissed Mom on the cheek and ran to the car before Travis could change his mind. I climbed in the back and hoped he didn't decide to be a total asshole and go to Madaket beach. It was the farthest one from the house.

Not even a couple of minutes later he pulled the car into a driveway and honked the horn. Seriously, my brother clearly had lost all semblance of manners living with his friends in a small New York City apartment while they all attended NYU.

A tall good looking guy sort of jogged toward us from the back of the house.

"Who's that?" I asked. We were at the Wells house. I didn't realize Travis was picking up more than Holden. Maybe I wouldn't have wormed my way into getting a ride if I was going to have to put up with more of them.

"Are you blind? That's Holden."

I had a hard time believing Travis. Holden was tall and gangly with stooped shoulders and hair that looked like he never washed it. The guy about to climb in the car was tall, maybe taller, and had wide football player shoulders, thick with muscles. The biceps on his arms strained the sleeves of his tee. He smiled and, wowza. He had perfect cheekbones, perfect teeth, a healthy tan, and handfuls of messy dark hair.

I had to blink a few times to get my eyes to stay in my head. I hadn't seen Holden for a few summers, boy had he changed.

I chewed on my lip and tried not to blush when he got in the car. He paused as he climbed in and looked at me. His gaze went from my head to my knees and back up. With a wink, he grinned and said, "How you doin'?"

I gulped hard as he slid into his seat and buckled in.

"Bruh, don't be gross, that's my sister," Travis complained.

Holden turned around and looked at me and then at Travis. "Bullshit, that's not Makenzie. Makenzie doesn't have curves. What's your name? When did you start dating this loser?"

"Um, Holden, yeah," I couldn't help but giggle. "I'm Makenzie and dating Travis would be gross. You know, he's, my brother."

"Bullshit!" He kept twisting to look at me and then Travis.

Travis just shook his head and rolled his eyes at us.

"Really, Makenzie? You grew up."

"Why is it such a shock that I grew up? You grew up too, and you don't see me acting all shocked."

I was stunned. I just wasn't going to let him, or my brother see me react like a love-struck fool.

Travis pulled the car over and cut the engine. Holden climbed out and held the door open for me.

"She can get out of a car on her own, come on," Travis said.

"Are you staying all summer, or are you jetting off to Europe?" Holden asked.

"Holden, drop it. Mak, you know the deal."

"Yes, I will leave you alone. You go that way"— I pointed in one direction, and then hitched my thumb over my shoulder, pointing behind me— "and I'll go in the opposite direction. I'm not seven anymore, Travis. I don't need you to play with me."

I spun on my heel and started a few steps down the beach. A second later Holden was tugging on the towel I had around my neck.

"What?" I asked as I spun to face him. In the distance behind him, Travis was already walking in the other direction.

Holden held out a chair to me. "You might want this."

"You aren't giving me your chair, are you?"

"No, there were four in the trunk. Hey, Makenzie, you know, I'll play with you if you want."

It was physically impossible to hide the blush that flared across my cheeks. Never in a hundred years would I have thought that Holden Wells would be someone I would want to play with. And by play, I meant touch, and possibly kiss, and more.

"I don't think my brother would like it very much."

"I don't want to take your brother out." His grin made my knees go weak.

"Holden Wells, are you asking me out?"

"Dude, come on. Leave her alone, or she'll get ideas and come hang with us!" Travis yelled up the beach.

"I sure as hell am not asking him out. Yes Mak, Makenzie"— he corrected, and my mouth went dry— "I'm asking you out. Travis doesn't have to know, not until we decide."

That night I told my parents I met a girl on the beach, and I was going to go meet Heidi for dinner at the Country Club. They never questioned a thing. They were just glad I had a friend on the island to hang out with. They never suspected there was no girl named Heidi, and that I was sneaking off to see Holden.

4

HOLDEN

A year and a half later...

T ravis let out a loud groan.

"What was that all about?" I asked.

Travis held up his phone. "Mom just texted. Mak is headed into town. I have to entertain her."

I stretched back on the couch and closed the laptop in front of me. I suppressed a grin. For the past year and a half, Makenzie had been finding more and more reasons to visit New York. The excuses were for her family and for Travis. I knew exactly why Makenzie was coming to New York and it had nothing to do with shopping or museum research.

"She always shows up when I want to party. It's like she's psychic or something," he complained.

"Or something," I confirmed. Less like she had psychic abilities, and more like someone was telling her exactly when he would be out of the apartment for the weekend.

Travis still didn't know that Makenzie and I had been seeing each other. It started off as fun, especially the keeping it secret part. At some point we got serious. Really serious, and the keeping it secret part was for self-preservation.

"She's trying to ruin my senior year experience," Travis said.

I let out a heavy breath. Travis had pulled some crappy stunts in regard to his sister. He was lucky Makenzie didn't have a vengeful bone in her body. She wasn't plotting ways to make Travis's life miserable; he was taking care of that himself.

"I've got a big exam next week. I'll hang out with her and study. Stop being so dramatic."

Travis dropped his hand on my shoulder and squeezed. "You are a hero among men. Thanks for taking one for the team."

I shrugged his hand off my arm. "Whatever."

The next day Makenzie arrived, and I had to pretend that I had no interest in her. All I could give her was a nod in greeting. It was a stab in my gut every time we did this. I could see her, I could sneak smiles and winks, but it was killing me that I could not pull her into my arms and cover her face with kisses.

"I'll help you with that," I said as I picked up her bag.

"She is capable of carrying her own shit. You can have my room. I won't be here," Travis said.

"You don't have to leave because I'm here. I can stay in a hotel. It's not like we can't afford it," Makenzie said.

"Where do you think I'm going? Look Mak, I promised Mom you could stay here. And we both know you don't need me to keep an eye on you. I mean, all you're doing is wandering around boring museums."

She reached out to try to take her bag from me. I shook my head. Doing my best to look like I wasn't interested, I left Makenzie and Travis bickering and hauled her bag to his room. A few moments later she came in and I locked the door behind her.

I pulled her into my arms and captured her lips with mine. I didn't need to say hello, I needed this. Her mouth was so pliable, so hot. Her tongue darted between my lips, and I twined my tongue with hers. I had Makenzie in my arms, and everything was better.

"Hi," her voice was breathy, and her smile went straight to my cock.

"Hi yourself. I have to get out there before he comes looking for me. He's taking off for a party, he'll be gone. Dave unofficially moved out about two weeks ago, so it's just us all weekend."

"Excellent timing. It's almost like someone told me there was a party this weekend that Travis would be going to."

I unlocked the door and left her with one more quick kiss. I picked up my laptop and pretended to study. It was a fight to keep my gaze on the monitor in front and not watch Makenzie move around.

"Will you have time for dinner together before your party?" she asked her brother.

He made complaining sounds that meant no.

"Look, we should at least send mom a picture of us together. Can you pretend to not hate me long enough to do that?"

I watched as they pasted fake grins on their faces and looked at the phone held in Makenzie's outstretched arm. They took the selfie and then Travis grabbed his keys and left without saying much.

Makenzie stared at the closed front door.

I did too. I also held my breath and started counting. How long would it take for Travis to turn around if he needed something? How soon before we didn't have to worry?

"Makenzie?"

She looked over her shoulder at me and shook her head before returning to stare at the door.

"Ten minutes," she said.

I set a timer on my smartwatch before I got off the couch and wrapped my arms around her shoulders. If she needed to stare at the door for ten minutes, then we would stand there and watch the door handle until Makenzie felt confident that Travis had left us alone.

The alarm on my watch beeped, and Makenzie relaxed in my embrace. With a sigh, she turned and melted against me. I stroked her hair as the tension eased out of her body. She shuddered in my arms, and I hated that her brother did this to her, was doing this to us.

"Promise me we can tell my family about us soon? I'm getting tired of sneaking around. At some point, my mother will call one of my professors at Mary Brooks and find out that my grades are not the greatest, and that there are no research projects sending me into the city."

"I graduate in a few months; we can see how things play out over the summer. At the very latest, we wait until you graduate. It's only another year, and then we can be open with everyone."

She sighed and backed out of my arms. "I know, I get it. Travis can be such an asshole. And I wouldn't put it past him to purposely mess up your studies."

"Hey," I hooked my finger under her chin and tilted her head so that I could look into her eyes. "I love you. I promise this hiding behind everyone's back will not last much longer. It will be worth it. We are worth it."

"I love you, Holden, and I trust you. I cannot wait to see Travis's face when he finds out and he can't do a damn thing about it." She let her arms lift over my shoulders and hooked her hands around my neck.

I let my hands skim down her sides and rest on her luscious hips. She wiggled in a little closer.

"He'll bust a gut," I chuckled. "I want to marry you, Makenzie. And I'm not going to let whatever stick Travis has up his ass get in my way."

"You want to marry me?"

"Do you honestly think we are doing all of this for a few dates? Of course, I want to marry you. After you graduate, we can get engaged. We can do the whole marriage thing, and then have kids."

"But not yet. I would be honored to have your babies Holden." She sighed into me and lifted herself up on her toes.

Her mouth was on mine again. I was going to make her my wife, and it was going to piss Travis off. He'd get over it. I pulled her to me, letting my fingers dig a little deeper into her softness.

She moaned into my mouth and pressed her breasts against my chest. As she pressed into me, I backed up until my legs brushed against the edge of the couch. I folded back and pulled her down with me. She shifted and wiggled against my body as our mouths twisted and pressed together.

My body responded as it always did when we were together. She did things to my body, to my mind. I hitched my leg over hers and rolled. We spun and she was under me. I hitched her leg over mine, palming her ass and thigh through the leggings she wore.

I pressed my hips against her, and she ground against my erection. Making love to Makenzie was a deliciously satisfying endeavour. The way she responded to my kisses and my touch was magic. It was a gift that I hoped she would be willing to give me for a long time.

She tugged on the hem of my tee. I didn't want to stop kissing her, but I had to stop long enough to pull the shirt off. The look on her face as she looked over me made my cock throb harder. Her fingers tickled over my skin.

"Bedroom?" I asked.

"I love you," she said with a nod.

5

MAKENZIE

A few months later, mid-May...

I once heard a song that complained about how miserable a hot summer was in the city. The few days around Travis and Holden's graduation were compounded misery. The temperature was hot, the company was miserable, the song was right.

Every time Holden and I were in close proximity we had to pretend we tolerated each other's company. And we were in proximity a lot. Our parents were friends. We did everything from pre-graduation brunch to attending the ceremony to post-graduation dinner together.

After the ceremony, we had to stand around in the heat waiting for Travis and Holden to find us. Mom was shaking with excitement when she saw Travis approaching. She started to reach out to welcome him in a congratulatory hug.

A loud squeal interrupted Mom's trajectory and some well-dressed co-ed launched herself at my brother. She planted a kiss on him, and he seemed to consume her face. The stunned look on Mom's face distracted me from seeing Holden as he strode up.

When I finally did see him, he had a huge grin on his face and was shaking his father's hand.

"Congratulations." Mom hugged Holden before Travis had managed to detach himself from the woman he was kissing.

Since Mom hugged him, I didn't think it would be a big deal if I gave Holden one too. After all, he had graduated. I had known him for years, no one would suspect anything.

I wrapped my arms around his neck. Holden wrapped one arm around me.

"Congratulations," I whispered into his ear. "I love you."

His lips grazed my cheek, and then I was alone on my own two feet.

Travis joined us, his girlfriend under his arm. "Everyone, this is Eve. Eve, these are my parents."

Eve was in the way, and I could tell Mom was disappointed that she was only giving her son a side hug.

"Will you be joining us for dinner, Eve?" Mom asked.

Travis had said nothing about having a girlfriend. Every time she was out of earshot, my mom was talking in low angry whispers. How dare he not tell us she would be joining us? Would she be coming to Nantucket as well? This was family time; was there anything she needed to be made aware of?

It gave me the opportunity to flirt a little more openly with Holden since Travis was distracted. At the end of dinner, we had to say goodbye.

"See you in a week," he whispered after he grabbed me in for a hug.

I left with Mom and Dad the next day for the summer house on Nantucket. Travis, without Eve, would be there in a few weeks. He had a big interview before he could join us.

I had to wait even longer for Holden.

"I'm going to head to the beach," I told Mom.

It was another day that I was going to sit and stare at my phone waiting for a text message from Holden letting me know he was on the island. I didn't want to do it while hiding out in my room avoiding Travis. And I didn't want to keep checking my phone where Mom would ask me why.

I took the car and parked next to the beach. I checked my phone.

"Landed."

I couldn't stop smiling. I put the car back into drive and headed straight to the airport.

Holden was waiting for me.

He slid into the passenger seat and immediately kissed me. "My parents aren't here yet. Want to fool around?"

I giggled and smacked his leg. "You are incorrigible. And yes, I want to fool around. It's been forever, and I've missed you."

He squeezed my thigh as I drove.

"I've been about to bust. If you hadn't snuck down the week before graduation, I don't know how I would have survived. Makenzie, I have missed you."

The hand on my knee roamed and he stroked my arm and caressed my breast.

I wiggled as he tickled me. "Stop, you're distracting me."

"Then drive faster," he said as he leaned over and kissed my neck.

I drove faster. I couldn't stop laughing as we raced from the car and into his family's empty summer house. If I had been worried that maybe they were there, the dust coverings on the furniture eased my mind. Holden held my hand as we raced up the stairs and into his bedroom.

I fell against him as he tried to open the door. He held me close as he leaned against the door as it swung open.

"Of all the girls I thought about bringing up here."

"Shut up and kiss me."

He did, and more. His hands were on my body, and I wanted all of him. The thinness of my bathing suit under the cover-up I wore made it feel as if there was nothing between my skin and Holden's hands. With a few deft moves of those hands, Holden removed my bathing suit.

It took a bit longer for him to get rid of his clothes. Before he got rid of his pants, he pulled a condom from his wallet. As soon as he did it was a reunion of our skin. My breasts against his chest, my fingers caressing him. His hands holding and kneading my thighs, my butt, my breasts.

Holden's lips claimed mine, and I returned the pressure. I nibbled at his lower lip until he let out a low moan.

"Makenzie, I have missed this."

"I love you," I told him.

We lowered onto the bed. Holden pressed me down against the mattress. I wrapped my legs around his hips. His cock was hard and hot as he stroked it against my pussy. I was more than wet enough, ready for him.

I fumbled for the condom packet and tore it open. Holden lifted onto his knees, presenting his beautiful, perfect cock to me. I rolled the condom down his length, reveling in the ability to touch this amazing man who loved me and let me love him.

I lifted my hips, encouraging him to stroke into me. Holden took his time, teasing my body. His kisses trailed across my jaw and down my neck. He cupped my breast in his hand and pinched my nipple between his fingers.

Whimpering, I arched against his hand. I threaded my hand into his hair and held his head to my other breast.

He teased and sucked my other nipple. Teeth scraped against the tender skin. It was perfect, it was what I needed from him. I rocked my hips. The only way this could be any more perfect was if he were in me, filling me.

With a groan, he shifted his hips and slid into me. I held on as he thrust into. I cried out with the pleasure that was Holden stroking into me. It was perfect.

We rocked, crashing our hips together. My focus was lost, and I saw stars as my body became overwhelmed with sensation. Holden continued to drive into me relentlessly.

"Holden, I can't, I can't..." I couldn't form words as everything clenched. My muscles threatened to seize in a riot of spasms that would overtake my system.

"That's it, keep going baby." Holden laughed as he held himself above me, pressing in over and over.

I fought the urge to not move, I wanted to lift my hips, to help Holden, to let him feel as good as I was feeling. I didn't know how much I was or wasn't able to do. The orgasm rolled me under like a wave washing over the shore. I saw lights and had to fight to gasp for breath.

The way Holden touched me was beyond magic, beyond perfection. The rhythm of his thrusts was a stark contrast to the inconstant twitching of my internal muscles. He continued to thrust until he pressed hard into me. The laugh in his voice turned to a roar as he came.

We lay tangled together until the afternoon light turned to twilight.

"I should head home," I said in a sleepy voice.

Holden tightened his arm around my middle. "Stay."

"You know I can't. I'm supposed to be at the beach."

"But instead, you're in bed with me, and I want to keep you. Can't you call your mom and tell her you're spending the night somewhere?"

"You mean like at Heidi's?"

"Who? Oh right, your pretend friend so we could sneak around. Yeah, why not?"

"But your parents?"

"My folks aren't showing up until the twentieth."

I sat up and stared at him. "Are you serious? Holden, today is the twentieth."

He shook his head. "No, it's not, it's the… oh shit. You've got to go."

I kissed him and pulled my bathing suit on. I was out the door and in my car faster than I knew I could move. I walked inside through the back door to our summer house a few minutes later.

"Oh, good, Makenzie, you're home. Run upstairs and get cleaned up. I'll need some help getting dinner together. The Wells will be over for dinner."

I gulped and tried not to stare.

"You know we always have a big dinner to celebrate the beginning of the season," she reminded me.

I smiled and skipped upstairs. I'd see Holden again in a few hours.

6

HOLDEN

Summer was going by entirely too fast. This was supposed to be the last summer before the start of my career and responsibilities. July was almost over. I never had enough time with Makenzie, even when we were home together. I wanted it to last forever. I felt responsibility rushing at me at a dizzying speed and there was no dodging it.

What had started as a random thought evolved into an idea. And instead of shrugging it off as a crazy thought like I typically would, I followed the idea up with some research and some conversations. A lot of conversations.

When I couldn't be with Makenzie, I found myself doing a lot of thinking down on the beach. The Fourth of July came and went, and my plan seemed even more important. Makenzie wasn't going to like my idea, but she was smart, she would see that in the end, everything would work out to our advantage. Mom wasn't going to be a fan of it either.

I didn't want anyone to try to talk me out of it. I held off on saying anything until everything was a done deal. I signed my name on the dotted line and committed.

Even though it was summer, Dad was at his desk with his head down studying a report. Mom's charity planning was on hold, and I didn't crack open a single book, we were on vacation. Even though we took the entire summer on Nantucket as a family, Dad didn't stop working. Dad never stopped working; it was going to be the death of him.

I wrapped my knuckles on the door frame to his office.

He looked up and ran a hand through his hair. He looked older than I remember him ever looking before. It's not like his hair was fully gray or anything, but the lines around his face weren't so fine anymore. He looked perpetually tired. Maybe that was age, maybe there was something stressing him out.

"Holden, come in. What has you darkening my door? You don't typically knock, so I assume something is bothering you?"

Dad was right, if I wanted something I usually strolled in, asked what I needed to ask, and then strolled right on out again. I stood in front of his desk. Part of me thought about how I should be standing, and when would I start naturally saying 'sir.' But I wasn't in the military, not yet, and Dad had never been as strict as his father had been.

"I was thinking about the future," I started.

A knowing grin crossed Dad's face and he began nodding. I could tell by the smirk what he was thinking. Only this time he wasn't right.

"You've met a girl. It was bound to happen sooner or later. Are you serious about her?"

I lifted my hands and pressed my palms out in a double stop gesture. I had met a girl and even though I had known her for most of my life, I don't think I actually met her until about two years ago. I was as

38

serious as I could be about her. But this wasn't about Makenzie, this was something else entirely.

I shook my head. "No girl at the moment." Lying about our relationship was a little too easy. "I've been thinking about something that I need to do. I'm tired of paying lip service to my convictions, and in honor of Grandfather and this great country we live in, I've joined the Army."

Dad's face changed from a knowing smirk to no emotion whatsoever. He stood slowly and walked around to the front of his desk. Even in shorts and dock shoes, he had the edge of serious business around him. With his arms crossed, he seemed to study me, assess my abilities, and reason.

"I thought after a few years of being a pilot, you would work for me."

"I know. But the more I thought about it, the more I realized I wasn't needed as a commercial pilot. I can be of more value, and fulfill my destiny in the Army. And when I get out, I'll have more expertise and be able to contribute to the business more."

"You know you don't have to be a pilot to have expertise. I thought you wanted to fly!"

"I do, I will. I've already met the basic requirements to be a pilot for the Army. I've got over twelve hundred flight hours. With my degree, I'm walking straight in as an Aviation Officer. After basic training, I'm hitting helicopter training."

"This is going to break your mother's heart. I think she wanted you around as her little boy for a while longer."

"I'm not a little boy, haven't been for a while."

Dad nodded. "You've been taller than me since you hit sixteen. You don't need to tell me. Though I really had thought this would be about a girl."

"I'm not ready for that kind of commitment. At least not yet."

Dad stood and clapped me on my shoulder. "When you are, you talk to your mother. I think she has a ring for you to use."

I rubbed the back of my neck. "I'm sure she does."

"How soon do you leave?"

"I need to be at Fort Benning in ten days."

Dad hissed through his teeth. "Ten days, that doesn't give us much time."

"I didn't want to give anyone time to try to talk me out of it. My mind's made up."

Dad put his hand on my shoulder. "I guess we should go tell your mother."

He guided me from his office and onto the back patio where Mom was sunbathing.

I expected her to be disappointed, mad even. I hadn't expected her to cry.

"But I don't understand."

"It's not for us to understand, Jeanette. It's our job to support his decisions." My dad had his arms around her. "He's a grown man."

"He's, my baby!" Mom pulled out of Dad's embrace and pulled me into one of her own. She held me like a small child. It was kind of awkward since I was well over six feet, and she was barely five and a half feet tall.

"It will be okay, Mom, I promise. I'm going in as an officer, and straight to flight training. I've put a lot of thought into this."

"So, you didn't get some girl pregnant and are skipping town to avoid her shot-gun-wielding father?"

I had to laugh. "No, nothing like that."

"You couldn't have given us more time?"

"The summer is already almost over. I'd be leaving for a job either way," I pointed out.

"You won't be able to summer with us."

"Mom, if I had a job, I wouldn't be able to summer with you," I explained.

"I don't understand why you think you need to have a job, a career? There is no reason for you to work, and you know that. Powell, tell him."

"He's well aware of that, Jeanette. A man has to have something to occupy his mind. You don't want Holden to do nothing. He can't sit by and idly twiddle his thumbs."

"He could play golf."

"I don't like golf, Mom. It's not the end of the world. Everything will be okay."

"I don't see what the point of trust funds having available if you're going to just go out and get a job?"

She insisted that I hug her one last time. At least for the afternoon.

"Will you be back for dinner?"

"Probably not tonight, Mom. But I will be here in the morning. I'm going to head out and find Travis. I haven't told him yet."

"How do you think he'll take it? You've done everything together since you've been in school."

I shrugged. "It's not like we were going into business together. He's going to go work in some New York skyscraper and that's never been for me."

"Good luck, son." Dad clapped me on the shoulder before I left.

This was harder than I had thought it would be. My recruiter had warned me it would be hard. It had been his idea to limit the time I had left. He had even suggested that I break the news the night before I was scheduled to leave.

I couldn't do that, that wasn't enough time. I still needed time to get used to the idea. Mom and Dad needed time. It wouldn't be fair. As it was, ten days were barely going to give me time to properly tell Makenzie goodbye. I wasn't sure there would ever be enough time to tell Makenzie goodbye.

I pulled out my phone and typed in a message.

I waited for her reply. I sat in my car and waited for her text to tell me where to meet her.

My phone buzzed and I looked at her message. I shook my head. We wouldn't be able to be alone, but there would be no chance of running into either of our families.

It would have to do.

7

MAKENZIE

Everything about this summer was going by so fast and I was terrified I was going to miss something. Miss a moment with Holden, a moment of joy where we could sneak away and be together. I was so concerned about missing something fun that it was the end of July before I realized I had missed my period. I couldn't remember the last time I had it. Fortunately, drugstores sold pregnancy tests, and they're cheap, fast, and easy. I had two purple lines telling me I needed to have a serious talk with Holden.

I couldn't wait. Two purple lines meant our timetable would move up. Two purple lines and we wouldn't have to keep hiding; we could tell people that we were in love and that we were going to get married because we were going to have a baby.

My phone buzzed, startling me.

"Can I see you?" Holden texted.

"Meet me at the ferry." We had been sneaking away on the ferry to Martha's Vineyard for the past two summers. It gave us time to be together where we could talk uninterrupted.

"Hi, beautiful," he said as he easily strolled over to me, his hands in his pockets. He looked so relaxed. He reached up and brushed a wind-whipped hair from my face. His grin was soft, and he looked tired.

"What's up with you? Good call on the ferry. I have something I want to talk to you about."

"Really? That's fabulous. I have something I want to tell you as well." I grabbed his hands and I skipped up the gangplank after we had our tickets in hand.

We found a bench that overlooked the water and waited for the engines to thrum to life and cast off. Holden started to speak but I put my fingers on his lips. Wait, wait. We hadn't cast off yet. And he knew my fears and always catered to my wishes when it came to waiting, to making sure we were alone. The island got smaller behind us as the ferry chugged its way over to Martha's Vineyard.

"Okay. I have something I need to tell you," I started.

"Let me go first."

"Oh, okay. I guess so. Are you alright?" I pushed down my enthusiasm.

Maybe he had a job. The look on his face had me worried that he wasn't going to be nearby for weekends together. If he wasn't going to be in New York it was going to be much more complicated. He could always come up to see me in Vermont. Mary Brooks College was in a tiny little town with only one hotel. If I was seen going in and out of that hotel with a man everybody at my school would know about it. But if I was engaged, publicly engaged, I wouldn't have to worry about that.

I bit my lip and quelled my excitement and waited for him to tell me what he needed to share.

Holden's brow furrowed and he looked deep into my eyes. It was like he was trying to search for an answer without asking me a question.

As much as I wanted to know exactly what he was thinking, all I could see was the beautiful depths of his eyes.

"What is it? Can you tell me? Did you get a job?"

"Kind of a job," he said.

"That's fabulous. Are you going to be flying?"

He shook his head and shrugged. "Sort of, no. Yes. It's not that kind of job."

"You're not going into finance with Travis, are you?"

Oh God, I hoped he wasn't. I didn't want to have to deal with Travis any more than necessary. It was bad enough that he was my brother. It was terrible that he was Holden's best friend. Travis was the quintessential I hate my sister kind of brother. He did what he could to make my life difficult. I didn't want him getting in the way of my future with Holden.

"Okay, so you've kind of got a job."

"I'm going to have to leave."

"You're moving, when?" I asked tentatively.

He nodded. He picked up my hand and squeezed it hard. A knot formed in my middle, and I no longer had to purposefully keep my enthusiasm down. It had left on its own.

"I can see that you're going to hate this."

"Then why are you doing it?" I winced at the whine in my voice.

His expression dropped; he was sadder than normal. "Dammit, this is harder than I thought it was gonna be. I mean, I'm just going away for the job. I'm not leaving. I'm not breaking up with you." "Okay," I said. That didn't sound good, but what else was there to say?

"I leave in ten days."

I blinked hard and looked at him with disbelief. Ten days? I didn't know what else to say. I kept saying okay, like some kind of an idiot. All other words and thoughts got stuck in my chest.

Holden stared at my hands in his. "I love you."

I slipped my hand from his and cupped his cheek. The scruff of his beard, not quite grown in, tickled my palm. He was scaring me, but I could do this for him. For us, for our unborn child.

"Whatever it is, we'll figure it out. We've survived this long sneaking around. We can keep going. What kind of job did you get? Where are they sending you?"

He lifted his gaze to meet mine again and that's when I knew that whatever it was, I wasn't gonna be seeing him anymore. It wasn't that he wanted to break up with me but that he had to because it wasn't just a job.

"I've joined the Army."

I bit the inside of my cheek hard trying to stop the tears. No, no, I didn't understand why. What was he saying?

"You did what?"

"I joined the Army." His voice got quiet, a sure sign that he was getting angry. "It's the right thing to do. I can't call myself a patriot and expect someone else to do the hard work."

"But Holden…" I didn't know what else to say.

"I'm going in as an officer. I go straight to officer training and aviation school."

"Aviation school? So, you are going to be a pilot."

"The Army has pilots?"

He let out a forced chuckle "Yes. The Army has pilots and aviation officers. I'll be flying helicopters."

"Okay. So, you go away for how long? What happens to us?" I couldn't believe what I was hearing.

"I get leave and we can write. There's the telephone. I'm not going to be completely out of touch. I won't be able to do much for the first eight weeks of training. That's the boot camp part."

"Right." All I could do was sit and nod.

"But once that's through and I'm into regular officer training courses I can call, I can write to you. I will write to you." He looked so earnest. He believed his own words.

"I just go back to school and wait for you exactly how long? I don't think it's going to be a little bit more than a year before we can do anything about us. It sounds like you've put a lot of thought into it. And it's what you really want to do."

He nodded. I bit my lip again and leaned against him. I couldn't help it, but that's when I started crying. I couldn't tell him about the baby. I couldn't find the words that would make him not do what he needed to do.

"Okay. Okay." There it was. I was saying okay, again.

I twisted my fingers into the fabric of his shirt. I sniffed back tears.

"Makenzie." He stroked my hair.

I scooted so that I was sitting on his lap. I let him hold me for the rest of the ride. Every now and then like a babbling idiot, I would just say okay, okay. I don't know if it was more to remind myself that it would be okay, or if I was telling him, it would be okay.

"Okay. Okay."

With each mile closer the ferry got to Nantucket, Holden got a little further away from me.

When he leaned in to kiss me, I flinched back. I was too sad. I couldn't. There was no us anymore. By the time I got home, I was a slobbery crying mess. Of course, the first person I literally walked into was Travis. I smacked into his chest as he was coming out the back door.

"What the fuck is wrong with you?"

I didn't think and blurted out, "Holden is leaving me."

"What?"

"Holden's leaving." I cried and then ran up to my room.

Travis followed and stormed into my room. "What did you mean when you said Holden was leaving you?"

I stared at my brother and with all the anger I felt for Holden that I could not unleash on the man who was causing me the pain, I yelled at Travis.

"We've been seeing each other for two years, and he is leaving to join the Army. He's not waiting for me to finish school like he promised. That's what I meant when I said Holden was leaving."

"What did you do? Why is he leaving?"

And like that Travis turned everything on its end. Like it was my fault that Holden was leaving.

Travis spun on his heels and slammed my door behind him, leaving me alone.

8

HOLDEN

I hated how sad Makenzie was. But she was a smart woman, and she knew that this was what I had to do. The entire ferry ride she sat in my arms, constantly muttering, 'Okay.' Telling herself that she would be fine.

And she would be. We weren't breaking up. This wasn't the end of us. This was going to let us grow up so that we took responsibility for our relationship as adults and not as kids playing at being adults.

I drove around the island, thinking, not certain where I was headed. I didn't exactly want to go home, and I needed to give Makenzie some space and time to realize things were not over between us.

I pulled over at a beach and got out. I started walking up the beach, not sure what to think. I knew I was making the right decision, but I hated seeing my mother and Makenzie so sad. The ferry ride to Martha's Vineyard and back hadn't given us enough time, and I knew I could get Makenzie to understand if I could just explain. I needed more time to talk to her, and she needed more time to realize things weren't as bad as she was thinking they were. Ten days suddenly seemed too soon, and even if I had a month, it wouldn't be enough.

My phone buzzed. My chest tightened, and my breath quickened. I looked at it, expecting it to be a text message from Makenzie telling me she was sorry that she overreacted, and telling me that she wanted to see me again.

I was surprised and a little disappointed when it was Travis.

"A little birdie gave me some news. We should meet up. Come find me at McIntyre's pub."

I guessed he had found out from Makenzie. Unless there was something else that he heard that I didn't know yet.

I texted a quick reply and got in my car.

McIntyre's was one of those fake old Irish pubs with dark wood paneling on the walls. It was the kind of place that served deep-fried fish with french fries and called it fish and chips. Other hit menu items included shepherd's pie and sausage with mashed potatoes, and a few more that people would expect to find in Ireland. They served Guinness and that's what mattered the most.

"What's up, man?" I said as I slid into a booth opposite Travis. There was already a nice, tall, perfectly poured pint of Guinness waiting for me.

Travis lifted his glass and tilted it in my direction. "This is to you, future Army man."

"I guess Makenzie told you I've joined the Army," I said.

"Yeah. Don't tell my sister secrets. She can't keep them."

"What else did she tell you?" I thought Travis would be pissed if he knew I was dating his sister. I also figured he'd get over it. He was taking this really well. Maybe Makenzie hadn't told him about us.

He shook his head. "Nothing. Is there something else she shouldn't have told me?"

It was my turn to shake my head. "Just the Army. Going to fly copters."

"I didn't expect this of you. I expected you to go for the cushy life of a commercial pilot. You do realize that working is for chumps?"

"Says the man who has a job on Wall Street." I shook my head and took a long pull of my beer.

"Wall Street isn't working. Wall Street is managing my portfolio."

"And other people's portfolios," I added.

"Might as well make a commission on it."

"You know you got that one right."

I tipped my drink back toward him and we clinked glasses.

"This one is on me. We need to give you a good send-off. How long have you got?"

"Ten days and counting before I have to show up for boot camp."

"Ten days for your last hurrah. Wine, women and music, and then it's all yes sir no sir, and saluting people who were born beneath you. Are they gonna make you shave your head?"

"Hey, it's not like that. We all get the same opportunities in the Army, it equalizes us. They probably will shave my head." I ran my hand through my hair. Makenzie liked it a little longer, that was going to change.

"Are they gonna make you do one of those obstacle courses they always show in the movies?" Travis tossed out questions. Some of them I should have asked my recruiter.

"I have no idea what they are going to put me through. I've got to do some basic training and then it's officer training.

"Officer? Are you mister high and mighty?"

"Can't fly if I'm not an officer and can't be an officer unless I have that college degree."

"Degree is all taken care of. That's one box you can check off. When will we be seeing you again?"

I shrugged. "Not sure what kind of leave schedule I'll get. And the first one I definitely have to spend with my mother. She's a mess"

"Oh man, mothers but you gotta love them."

I agreed. "You gotta love them."

He bought another round, and we shared a basket of fries. We talked bullshit. Travis told me what he thought his future was going to look like.

"Is Eve going to be in it?" I asked.

He shook his head. "She hasn't bothered to come to see me on the island. Not once. She keeps saying she can't get time off from her job. If being with me was important, she would have found time."

I shook my head and ate another fry. "Not everyone can take their last summer off."

"Sure, sure. And some people need to work for a living. You think I should call her when I get back to the City?"

"I guess it depends on how much you like her and want to see her."

He shrugged. "There are more women out there, and I'm still young. Why saddle me with just one at this point?"

He stretched and leaned back.

"Remember when we were young, and girls were something neither of us was interested in?"

I laughed. "That was a long time ago. And that's changed."

"Are there women in the Army?"

"What kind of idiot question is that? Of course, there are women in the Army."

"Won't that be a distraction from flying?"

I shook my head. "I think you've had too much to drink."

"No, I'm good. One more, one last one." He signaled the waitress and ordered us another round of Guinness.

When the beer arrived, Travis stood and raised his glass high. "A toast to my best friend," he said loud enough to get the attention of the rest of the restaurant.

"Glasses up, I said a toast!"

The other people sitting at their tables raised their glasses.

"To Holden Wells as he joins the Army."

There was a general muttering in response to his toasts, and everyone took a drink. A few people made a point to come over and shake my hand.

"You've made the best decision of your life," one man said. He introduced himself as an Army veteran. "Where will you be stationed?"

"Not sure yet. I'm off to Fort Benning, officer training."

"Next time I see you, I'll have to salute you."

I was joining a brotherhood that would expand my horizons and give me purpose. We said our goodbyes, and he left with his party.

"Mr. Army man," Travis sneered.

"That's Officer Army man to you," I jokingly replied.

Travis slapped both of his hands onto the table and leaned forward. His face twisted into a grimace.

"I hope they shave your head and kick your fucking ass."

I flinched back. "What the fuck?"

"Makenzie told me everything, you asshole. I can't believe you've been fucking my sister of all people. She is stupid and you're ignorant. I hope you get what is coming to you."

He pushed to his feet.

I stared up at him in shock.

"If you ever touch my sister again, I'll cut your balls off and destroy your family's fortune. This one's on you," he said as he upended the pint on my head and walked out.

Beer dripped down my face. I guess I grossly underestimated his reaction to Makenzie and I dating.

My last ten days on Nantucket were spent being coddled by my mother and texting Makenzie. Only she never responded.

I vacillated between thinking I had made the biggest mistake of my life or maybe I had made the best decision I could have. On the one hand, I obviously lost Makenzie, and Travis had clearly walked away from me, and our friendship. On the other hand, what kind of man was he that he was willing to give up a life-long friendship because I was dating his sister?

The Underwood family showed me their true colors and it was clear that I no longer mattered to them. So, they no longer mattered to me.

9

MAKENZIE

Several months later, end of November...

I wheeled my suitcase toward my room. I had help with the few boxes I was moving back in.

"So, they finally kicked you out?" Travis leaned against the door frame to his old bedroom, arms crossed, a judging smirk on his face.

I stepped out of the way of the help and stared at him. I felt very little these days, so I'm sure my expression was empty, an emotional void.

"What?"

"Mary Brooks finally decided they wouldn't tolerate harlots in their student body. No unwed mothers, time to go?"

I shook my head. I don't know why I bothered explaining anything to him. But this was my choice. I ran a protective hand over my distended pregnant belly.

"I'm moving most of the stuff out of my dorm room. After Thanksgiving, I only have a few tests and then the semester is over. It seemed like a good idea to get moving out of the way early."

"Ah, so you're a dropout now?"

I started walking again, pushing my bag ahead of me. Let Travis think what he was going to think. It didn't matter. He would argue and disagree with anything I said or did, even if it was a money-making great idea. If I was involved, he predetermined it to be a bad idea.

When I found out I was pregnant at the end of July, back when my life was still wonderful and Holden still loved me, I was much further along than I could have realized. I was now closer to seven months along than to six, and with the baby due in February, there was no logistical way to complete my last semester and have a new-born. The workload would be too much.

With the advice of my parents, I decided to take the Spring semester off, and finish up the following summer. Of course, Travis would see that as dropping out of school.

I had to be more than perfect for him to see the value in anything I did. As much as I wanted to be independent and not rely on Travis to play with me just like when I was a little girl, I still really wanted my brother to like me. Those protective older brothers that were in the movies were completely fictional as far as I was concerned. My brother was determined to destroy my self-esteem. He didn't need to try very hard; my self-esteem was already tanked.

I walked into my old room. It seemed like the girl who had wanted a pink princess room was someone else, not me. Coming back to this room felt almost like losing, and somewhat foreign. I wasn't a little kid anymore, but here I was back in a little kid's room.

I sat on my bed, weary both mentally and physically. This baby was causing me all kinds of issues, constantly feeling tired was the most consistent of them. At least she was letting me eat without the constant morning sickness. Whoever said that lasted roughly for the first three months was a bold-faced liar. I didn't have any morning sickness until after the first trimester was over. And then it was morning sickness any time of the day or night, and heartburn, so much heartburn. I probably chewed down as many of those chalky tablets as I did real food.

The most recent issue this little one liked caused me to swell. If I was on my feet too long during the day, my ankles would swell. My fingers had started to swell, and I could no longer wear any rings.

Travis barged into my room. "Okay, future welfare queen, I'll pony up twenty grand if you tell me who the father is."

"Get out of my room Travis. Just because neither of us lives here full time anymore doesn't mean the rules about my room have changed. You didn't knock."

He stepped into the hall, knocked, and stepped right back in. "Happy now?"

That man twisted every rule to his advantage. He thought the world owed him what he wanted simply because he wanted it. But he had me for a sister, and I had learned at a young age to do my very best to not let Travis win simply because he thought he should.

I rolled my eyes, too tired to do much else. It was going to be a torturous long weekend with him here the entire time.

"Twenty grand, take it or leave it."

"Leave," I said.

"Fine, forty grand."

I stood and walked toward him. I grabbed his arm and swung him around and pushed him out of my room. "I don't need your money, Travis. And I'm not telling you."

The fact that he was too egotistical to figure out that Holden was my baby's father astounded me. Travis just couldn't put two and two together, because he couldn't accept that Holden would be interested in me.

I closed the door behind him and locked my door. The next time he knocked I ignored him.

Laying on the bed I curled up around my belly and cried, again. Between the hormones and the sadness over losing Holden, I cried daily.

I cried because I had given up the last few days I had to be with Holden in my selfishness. I cried when I wrote to him every week and he never responded. I cried when I thought about him and thought about writing but I didn't because what was the point? No matter what I wrote to Holden, he never responded.

My classes were a completely different set of stressors. It was my senior year and I had thesis papers to write. Research to conduct, and I was overwhelmed. I was barely passing my classes.

There was a knock on my door.

"Go away, Travis."

"It's Dad, not Travis."

I swung my legs over the side of my bed and sat up. "Give me a second."

I took my time crossing my room and opening the door.

Dad stood there with another box, a big one.

"What's that? All of my things are already in here." I gestured at the stack of boxes in the corner of my room. I stepped back to give him room to come in.

"This isn't yours, but it is for you."

He put the box down in the middle of the floor and turned it around so I could see the label on the front.

"A crib?"

"Your mother picked it out. We thought about giving it to you as a Christmas present but realized the baby is reason enough. I thought Travis and I—"

"Travis isn't going to help. You know how he is," I said.

"I think you underestimate your brother."

"You overestimate him. He hates me, Dad. He might help you with the crib, so he can do something with you. He won't be doing it for me."

Dad shook his head.

I knelt down and looked at the picture on the box. It was pretty, and it would look beautiful set up in here. "I'm going to need to pick out bedding."

I looked around the room, maybe princess pink wasn't such a bad color choice if I was having a girl.

"Your mother wanted to surprise you with bedding as well, but we don't know if you're having a boy or a girl yet."

"Well, neither do I. I do love it. Thank you." I sat all the way back onto my butt and cried.

Dad awkwardly patted me on the shoulder. A crying daughter wasn't something he had dealt with much; Mom was the one who usually handled my tears. I leaned against his leg.

"When your mother was pregnant, she would cry at everything. It's perfectly normal."

I wiped my tears. "Thanks, Dad. Help me up?"

I held my hand up to him.

With a grunt and a heave, he pulled me to my feet.

"I'm going to go find Mom and tell her I love the crib. Maybe she will want to go shopping for the bedding?"

"Does your mother ever turn down an opportunity to go shopping?"

Dad wasn't wrong, but the shopping I had in mind wasn't high up on Mom's list of fun. I wanted to head out to the fabric shop. I suddenly had an urge to use my sewing skills to learn how to make a quilt, and a baby quilt seemed like the perfect first project.

1 0

HOLDEN

4 years later...

I stood at the back of the hangar, in the office, and watched the group of trainees as they waited for me. I learned shortly after I started my assignment of being a flight trainer that observing how the young officers behaved before I stood in front of them was valuable for finding out who were the hotshots, the ones who fought for the alpha position of the cohort.

Those were the pilots who would question my directions and push the limits. They thought they were natural leaders. Sometimes they were, sometimes they were just assholes. I wanted to have an idea of which ones I could expect to have to deal with. I would have to cultivate their ego into precision and action. I needed pilots who could fly into dangerous situations and fly right back out.

A cocky attitude and an inflated ego were not always beneficial in those situations. Cool heads and analytical reasoning were stronger traits when it came to piloting in combat.

My trainees sat in rows of folding chairs behind folding tables set up in front of a Blackhawk and a whiteboard. My classroom was in the wide-open space of an aircraft hangar. We took up only a small portion of an active, functioning aircraft hangar. We were right in the middle of everything. Being able to focus, learn, and function amidst chaos and heat and humidity was all part of the plan.

My students cut up with each other and were relaxed. They had come from all over and hadn't met each other until this morning. But that didn't stop the instant camaraderie, and sometimes, ego-fed antagonism. This lot seemed to lean towards being friendly. It didn't mean that I wouldn't butt heads with a bad attitude, but it was promising. I couldn't decide who were the overachievers, and who already knew it all.

I had reviewed the files of each one of the pilots before they were even allowed into my training class. But words on paper could not take the place of observation. My presence would change their demeanor. A good officer understood the personalities of his men, a good teacher understood his students. I strived to do both.

I took the long way around from the office, giving myself more time to study them. One of their ranks had been keeping an eye out for my arrival, and my presence was announced as soon as I decided it was time to join them.

"Officer on deck."

My students reacted instantly. Chairs scraped as they all stood at attention at my approach. I didn't even have time to salute or introduce myself before hell came raining down on us.

I can't say there was one thing that I learned in my years as an aviation officer and that was singularly more important than anything else. I can say the lessons of 'expect the unexpected,' and 'always be ready to react because you never know when you'll need to jump into action' were the two that managed to cross my mind in those first few seconds of the disaster.

I think I reacted more to the sound than to other stimuli. We had no warning. I had always thought there would be a few seconds where I would be able to assess and make choices. But that wasn't the case.

Everything happened all at once. There was a roar like a train, combined with a thunderous clap and metal screeching. There was yelling and screaming. It seemed like explosions surrounded us. Everyone's training took over and we all jumped in different directions. Everyone ran in a different direction, instinctually running toward the danger, only we were surrounded. I was knocked on my back and thrown across the floor toward the bird. That's what saved me. It's also what broke me. I didn't remember anything after that.

It was the softness of the bed and the smell that I reacted to first. The acrid burning smell had been replaced with the distinct antiseptic scent that was unique to hospitals and medical facilities.

I was awake and I didn't want to be. I groaned and struggled to open my eyes. My vision was blurry. The light seemed excessively bright. My mouth was dry, my tongue swollen and made of terrycloth. Beeps turned to screams as sensor alarms went off. Pain screamed into my head. Returning to sleep seemed like a good idea.

"Oh, good. Welcome back, Lieutenant. Can you tell me your name?" a nurse with a soft voice asked.

"Wells." It really hurt to talk. "Lieutenant Holden Wells."

"That's good enough for now. I don't need your full rank and serial number. Do you know what day it is? Can you tell me what happened?"

"No." I tried to push up into a sitting position, I didn't want to be on my back. I was suddenly aware that I was uncomfortable. My legs felt heavy, and one of my arms felt swollen. I was covered in sticky sensor leads and IVs.

I wasn't sure what had happened. I was about to meet my most recent training cohort, and then there had been explosions and screaming. I had no idea how long ago that had been. It could have been hours; it could have been days.

"Do you want to get up?"

"Yeah, please." My voice sounded even worse than it felt, and it felt horrible and scratchy.

With a whir, the back of the bed angled up, and without effort on my part, I was in a more upright position.

"What's the last thing you remember Lieutenant?" The nurse continued to ask questions as she rearranged pillows under my legs and arm. I was covered in thick bandages down one side of my body.

"Is this an interrogation? Do I remember who I am, where I am?"

"That's exactly what this is." The nurse continued to adjust my bedding and the IV.

"What happened to me? Where am I?"

"You'll get the details in a debriefing. But I can tell you that you're in the hospital. You've had two surgeries to repair a spiral fracture in your left leg and multiple breaks in your left arm. You've suffered multiple contusions, a concussion, and two fractured ribs."

"That explains why things hurt." And everything hurt.

I felt a gentle hand on my arm. "That's why things hurt. Now that you're conscious, let's see how long we can keep you awake before giving you more morphine. I'll let the doctor know you are awake."

Some point later a doctor came in and prodded me. Different nurses took my stats and gave me meds. I was on some serious pain medication and drifted in and out of consciousness. Awake and drugged out felt like floating in clouds. I was aware of my body, but it didn't hurt. And there was a veil of fog like mist surrounding my brain as if I couldn't see through it. Thoughts were skewed and fuzzy.

I didn't learn the full extent of the situation until after I had a debriefing several days later. A training exercise had gone horribly wrong. A pilot had to ditch his plane during landing. And that's when the aircraft went sideways, literally.

Instead of crashing into the empty tarmac, the aircraft cartwheeled and crashed into the far corner of the hangar where my class was being held. Support beams were sheared in half. The building collapsed right on top of us, and many others. An I-beam severed the tail section of the helicopter I ended under.

In the few days following surgery, I learned the extent of my injuries. Both bones on my forearm had snapped. My left leg suffered a spiral fracture in the tibia, the fibula had snapped, and there was a cluster of hairline fractures in my femur. I was held together with titanium plates, screws, and more pins than I could count. And I was one of the lucky ones.

The pilot that crashed survived, but a lot of the soldiers inside that hangar had not. We lost good men and women that day.

I was still struggling with balancing being conscious with the painkillers when I received the call. It took several hours before I fully grasped the enormity of what that call had meant. Part of me thought it had to be a drug-induced hallucination.

My father couldn't die. That was something I could not fully accept. I hadn't even had a chance to talk to him after my accident to let him know I was all right. I didn't even know if my parents had even known about the accident. And now the accident seemed inconsequential. My father was dead.

11

MAKENZIE

Present, six weeks after the funeral...

"Where do you want these?" Mom asked as she pulled open a case of ribbons.

"I think along that wall." I pointed to a large section of empty shelving that hadn't been designated for anything yet.

"I'm so proud of you, Makenzie. You took a dream, made it a plan. And look at you. You're really doing it."

"Thanks. But I couldn't be where I am right now without you. I couldn't do it without you. And I certainly couldn't do it without Gloria."

"I was surprised to learn that Gloria liked to quilt as much as you do. I never knew."

"Just because you don't like to do craft projects, Mom, doesn't mean your friends don't."

"I guess. She never mentioned it, we always talked about tennis mostly."

I shook my head. Mom talked about tennis to the exclusion of listening to other people.

"You act like it's such a strange thing to want to make quilts. It's making art and playing with fabric."

"I've never really understood art. Well, you have always been the creative type. After all, you studied Art History at Mary Brooks College."

I had graduated with a degree I wasn't sure how I would use. They didn't have programs in costuming or fabric arts; Art History was the closest option available.

When Gloria mentioned wanting to own and run a quilt shop, I jumped at the opportunity to go into business with her. And now we were setting everything up with plans of opening in a month.

I carefully slid the open blade of the box cutter down the middle of the tape on the large box in front of me. I couldn't just slam the blade down and rip open the box, I had to be careful of the contents. I gasped as the box opened revealing the treasure inside. Bolts and bolts of brightly colored quilting cotton, wrapped in plastic waited for me.

The lush colors and whimsical patterns made me happy just to look at them. I wanted to pet and play with the fabric immediately. If I stopped and did that every time a new shipment came in, this quilt shop would never get set up.

The front door opened.

"I'm sorry we aren't open for business," I said without looking up.

"I hope not. It's a bit of a mess in here." Gloria, my new business partner said. "Have you been getting a lot of walk-ins? Oh, is that the new Kate Bassett fabric?" She distracted herself when she saw the fabric piled next to me.

"Yeah, it's yummy, isn't it? I said, running my hand over the plastic-wrapped fabric that had begun to pile up on the massive white laminate cutting table in the middle of the shop.

"There's so much of it. I don't know what I'll make first. I think that's going to be both the best and the worst part about owning my own quilt shop. I'll be able to play with all the fabric, but then I'll be so sad I have to cut it into pieces and sell the fabric. I won't be able to take it home with me," Gloria said.

"Isn't that the whole point of opening the quilt shop so that we can share all of this with other people?"

Gloria nodded. "That and to have an excuse to buy bolts of fabric."

She picked up a bolt that I had just unloaded, a very modern take of a fairy tale design created in bright fuchsia and hot lime and other crazy, wonderful colors. Gloria held it as if it was a beloved teddy bear. "It's just so perfect. I've always wanted to be able to just buy a bolt of fabric and not know what I was going to do with it."

"Well, now you do know what you're going to do with it," I said. "You're going to sell it. And make as many sample quilts as you want."

For me, having all the supplies and all the fabric I wanted at my fingertips for creating was what appealed the most.

"Where do you want these?" Gloria's son Ethan grunted as he carried in an armful of boxes.

"Depends on what they are," I said.

"Those are the sewing machines for the classroom," Gloria said. "Put those in the classroom area."

"Where?"

She pointed to the back of the long room that was to become our shop. We hadn't finished determining the details of how the shop was going to be set up, but we had sectioned off the classroom area with a line of blue painter's tape on the wall and floor.

We still had shelving to assemble and other display furnishings to bring in. The front half of the space was going to be our retail shop with fabric and all the notions someone could possibly want for quilt making. The back third we were sectioning off for teaching space.

Gloria and I agreed we wanted to bring in big name designers for workshops. For the first year, we would be the ones teaching classes, but the plan was that as soon as we could, we would book someone from our personal wish list of designers we would love to study with.

"Does Nantucket really need another quilt shop? After all, how many people really sew?" Mom asked.

"You're a riot, Jennifer. It's not just little old grandmothers quilting. Kate Bassett is only in her thirties, and she's covered in tattoos. Her fabric is a limited edition, and after it's no longer available it sells for hundreds of dollars a yard. It's a whole subset of the industry."

Ethan grunted as he set another load of boxes down with a loud thump.

"Sh," I lightly chastised him. "Ainsley is napping, don't wake her up."

"Sorry Mak. She's out like a light," he said.

"You can never have enough quilt shops," I said, returning to the conversation.

Ethan joined us and leaned against the cutting table. "With Ainsley asleep, I can't start assembling the tables. What do you want me to do now?"

"I think you can take off for a few hours' sweetie. She won't be asleep all day."

Gloria ruffled his hair.

"You're such a good young man. I don't know how all of this will get set up without you," Mom bragged on him.

"Thanks." Ethan looked down at the ground. If he were any younger, I would have expected him to kick at something on the floor to avoid the embarrassment.

I agreed. Ethan was a good guy, but I didn't want to embarrass him further. "What are your plans for the rest of summer?"

"I don't know." He shrugged. "You'll need me plenty around here."

"But that doesn't mean you'll not have much time for other things, don't you?" I asked.

I looked back to where Ainsley was asleep in the playpen.

"What are you thinking, Mak?" Gloria asked.

I shrugged. It was a wild hair of an idea. "We still haven't settled in since the move, what with jumping right into opening the store. I haven't begun the process of hiring a nanny."

"I told you we can call the agency," Mom interjected.

"I know, but I still would need to interview the candidates from the agency and run my own background checks."

"We never worried about any of that when you were children. We simply trusted who they sent over."

"I know, you've said. But I'm not you, and I'm looking for hiring a long-term nanny, not a babysitter for the evening. There's a difference."

"I don't know how I would fit in there. I can't do the interviews for you."

"No, but you could be the nanny until I have time. I mean, Ainsley already likes you, you're good with her."

Ethan put up his hands in a double stop gesture. "I don't know about that."

"I'm willing to pay you the agency rates. And I don't know anyone else who would be looking for a job that would end when it's time to head back to school. Anyone I know would be on the island vacationing for the season."

Ethan looked back at the sleeping toddler. "Nanny? I don't want people to hear her call me Nanny."

"She doesn't have to call you nanny, it's a job title, not a name. If you can get her to call you Ethan, I'm good with that."

"A male nanny?" Mom asked.

"Childcare is not a gendered role. If Ethan thinks he might have kids someday, this will give him a leg up."

Gloria started giggling. "We could call you a Manny."

Ethan pulled out his phone and leaned back on the cutting table. "Were you serious when you said you'd pay me agency rates?"

He held out his phone to me. There was a number on the screen.

"This is what an agency that serves Martha's Vineyard is charging per hour. "Are you seriously willing to pay me this?"

Ethan's mother grabbed the phone from his hand and looked at the rate. "She is not paying you that much. That's ridiculous. The nannies at that agency make half that if not that much."

"But she said…"

I took the phone from Gloria and looked at the amount. I didn't know what I was expecting to pay, this did seem a little steep, but it is what I said I would pay.

"Yeah. It won't be a full-time job, because there will be times Ainsley can be here, and I will be nanny shopping once the store is open and running."

Ethan nodded. "Sounds like a good deal to me."

I held my hand out to him. He slid his hand into mine and we shook on it.

"How soon can you start?"

12

HOLDEN

Immediately following the funeral, I returned to base and began my recovery. Regaining my ability to move and walk had been more brutal than the accident. At least I didn't remember the accident.

When it was obvious that my injuries were going to impact my ability to fly, the Army decided to let me go. I had a discharge in one hand and a stack of legal documents for dealing with my father's death in the other hand.

I couldn't do anything about the discharge. I hadn't fully recovered my stamina, and I wasn't physically able to take on what I needed to do. It was a clear case, and I was out.

My physical therapist said my strength would return in time, and that I needed to take it slow, but I needed to continue working. Even if it was a tortoise's pace. A tortoise's pace still wins the race.

My physical therapist released me from care with a long list of instructions on how to continue my recovery on my own. I needed to expect to not be able to run or lift weights for quite some time. But I didn't need some medical professional with a clipboard telling me how to walk or hold a pencil.

I headed to Nantucket to open up the summer house for the season. I hoped it would give me the time I needed to get situated, both mentally and physically, without the added stress of having to be physically present at Dad's business offices.

Mom wanted me to go through dad's things. She didn't think she could face up to it herself. That meant I was going to be on the island alone. As an adult, it would be the first time I'd been alone for any length of time since I joined the Army straight out of college.

I would have to manage on my own clearing out my father's estate and saving what I thought Mom would want to keep. Her memories were hers and not mine to sort out, but I could go in and take care of some of the more obvious things of Dad's that would only cause her pain. I could easily clean out his old office and get rid of his summer clothes and golfing equipment.

It had been years since I was back, and after a week of rattling around the old house, I decided it was time to get out. I headed into town where someone walking slowly wasn't all that uncommon.

Nothing had changed. I didn't think anything on the island ever changed. I now mostly walked with a cane. My physical therapist back in Connecticut had warned me about becoming too reliant on one and wanted me to wean myself off. The plan was to start taking short walks cane-free, and gradually build up to longer and longer walks. Walking in town helped. The blocks were short, and I didn't want to be seen walking with a cane like some old man.

I had my driver park at the end of the block, planning a short walk, about halfway up the block and back. I moved slowly and took my time. It was still early in the season for there to be too many tourists as expected.

What wasn't expected was the woman at the end of the block coming out of a store. She was an angel and even more beautiful than the last time I saw her if that was even possible. Her long flaxen hair was pulled back into a half ponytail half-bun thing on the back of her head. She slid large, lensed sunglasses onto her face. She turned her head as if she was scanning the street. She hadn't seen me.

Disappointment lingered at the back of my neck as I realized I had wanted Makenzie to see me. Even though her brother had threatened me with bodily harm, as well as financial ruin if I so much as spoke to her. I knew that he was more full of shit as an adult than he had ever been while we were friends. An empty threat from Travis wasn't going to stop me. Not after what I had already been through.

I sucked in my core muscles, gritted my teeth, and walked with the smoothest gait I could possibly muster, trying to hide my obvious limp.

"Makenzie, I can't believe you're here."

She turned and her perfect mouth made a little O. I was flooded with memories of kissing that perfect mouth. Would I ever be allowed to kiss her again? I suddenly missed Makenzie in a way I hadn't realized I had been hiding from myself for years. The pain of it was practically physical.

"Holden? Oh my God, it's you. What are you doing here?" She reached out and leaned in to give me the most perfunctory of courtesy hugs that I had ever received. There was no crushing of her body to mine as there was no tilt of her chin seeking out a kiss. It was the hug of old friends. And that's it.

"I'm on the island to clean out my parents' house and go through my dad's things."

She rested one hand just below her clavicle and grabbed my hand with the other. She tilted her head, and if I could see her face behind those sunglasses, I would have seen concern in her eyes.

"I am so sorry about your father, Holden." She squeezed my hand. "I am so sorry I wasn't brave enough to walk up and say anything to you or your mom at the funeral. I didn't know what to say. I didn't think you needed someone else crying all over you when you were already hurt and grieving yourself. It's a decision I truly regret."

I tried to look into her eyes but all I could see was my own grimace reflected in her sunglasses. Maybe she really was sorry.

Makenzie had always been a girl with a big heart. She took on other people's pain too easily. As the young woman I had loved, that was one of her most endearing traits, her ability to have compassion for others. It wasn't hard for me to accept that she would have been too upset to speak to me at the funeral as she was doing now.

"I asked Travis to give you, my condolences. I hope he wasn't too much of a jerk about it."

I chuckled. Travis had indeed been too much of a jerk. "Travis did pass along your condolences and then he threatened me. Yeah, so I take it some things haven't changed, right?"

Makenzie shook her head. "I'm so sorry about that. Travis excels at getting more unlikeable every year."

I wasn't sure what to say next. I was okay just to stand there and look at her for a while. It had been far too long since I had seen her.

There was a clamor behind her, and she turned, dropping my hand like a hot potato. A young man wrestled a stroller through the door.

I couldn't tell how old he was. He could have been an old-looking nineteen or a young-looking thirty. Considering he was pushing a stroller and appeared to actually know what he was doing, I decided to err on the latter side.

"Mommy," the little girl in the stroller said. She was dressed in pink and frills. Makenzie stooped down and adjusted the child's hat.

She had the same little pointed chin and button nose Makenzie had. This was clearly her kid. I looked back at the man pushing the stroller and noticed he had similar fair coloring. He must have been the father, so older than he looked.

Cold water ran through my veins. Any thoughts that might have tickled the edges of my brain about pursuing her again retreated hard and fast. I needed to get out of there.

"Have a nice vacation," I said and lifted my hand in a half-assed wave.

"Oh, I'm not vacationing. I live here now. I moved to be here full time. If you're back on the island, I guess we'll be running into each other again, at least for the summer."

I nodded. I didn't know how I'd handle seeing Makenzie for the summer after so many years of trying to forget her. "Maybe we'll run into each other again."

I should have turned and walked away, but the muscles in my left leg started to quiver with fatigue. I needed her and her little family to walk away first. She handed something to the little girl in the stroller and muttered something to her husband, pointing down the street, away from where my driver waited in the parked car.

"I'll be seeing you around," she called out after me.

Standing in place, I nodded as she walked away. I fought for control over my muscles. I refuse to let her see me limping.

13

MAKENZIE

The shop was coming together slowly but surely. Another day, another case to unpack and populate the shelves. As the opening date of the shop loomed, it felt like very little progress was being made.

Ethan had finally finished putting together all of our furnishings. We were going with a bit of a different-than-expected look. This was not someone's grandmother's idea of an old quilt shop. We purposefully chose to not go with old country time style or even a more modern shabby chic style. We had taken a spin of mid-century modern crossed with heavy contemporary. Everything was stark white and chrome.

Personally, I thought it was perfect as it didn't distract from the kaleidoscope of fabrics on display. But half of our shelving units were still empty. We didn't have a cash register yet. Ethan still needed to assemble the long-arm quilting frame, and there were no sample quilts hanging on the walls. What was a quilt shop without quilts? Gloria had promised we would have plenty of sample quilts showing off the gorgeous fabrics we were going to sell and the fun quilt classes we were going to teach.

Someone walked past the front window. I caught a glimpse of dark hair in my peripheral vision. With a startled gasp I turned to look. Adrenaline evaporated from my system as quickly as it had flooded it. My shoulders drooped as I saw that it wasn't Holden.

"Get it together girl," I muttered.

It had been days since I had seen Holden. And I really wanted to see him again. Even if he hadn't seemed particularly happy to see me, I needed to see him. He looked good. There was obvious pain in his expression, but that was understandable since he was here to deal with his father's estate, plus recover from that horrible accident. He would always look good to me, even with a little extra wrinkling around his eyes or new furrows on his forehead.

As I unpacked a box of needles and other machine accessories, I twisted myself so that I could no longer see out the front window. If Holden walked by, he would have to step into the shop to get my attention. I needed to focus.

"The tablet came in!" Gloria announced as she walked in the door.

I turned to say something and knocked the box on the floor.

"That's fabulous." I followed the box down and began picking up the spilled packages of product.

We now had a way to create invoices and take credit cards. It was another step closer to being able to open the shop.

As I looked up to say something else, I caught sight of dark hair. This time it was Holden. A surge of excitement hit my nerves. I had to pretend to not be thrilled at the sight of him. I was so proud of myself that I didn't run out the door and grab him into a fierce hug.

The last time I had seen him, I had been too shocked to know how to act. This time I had to consciously stop myself from acting like a fool.

As I watched him move, I noticed something wasn't right. I slowly stood and crossed the store, stopping at the door. I looked through the window as he continued down the sidewalk. He walked with a pronounced limp, and his shoulders lifted as if he were wincing with pain. As he walked, he tugged the sleeve on the left arm of his shirt down, as if he were trying to cover something.

What had happened to him?

All I knew was that he had been in an accident. His injuries weren't combat-related, but he had still gotten them on the job. I guessed accidents happened even in the military. I sighed. I didn't want him in pain or struggling.

I kept biting my lower lip. He seemed fine the other day. But it made sense for him not to be. He had to have been so badly injured to have been wrapped up the way he had been at his father's funeral. Both his arm and leg had been in thick casts that looked more like bandages.

"What's going on? Is something happening outside?" Gloria asked.

I shook my head. "No, I thought I saw something. Must have been a reflection of a car going by."

But I hovered at the door, watching. Holden moved with slow, precise actions. He didn't look particularly stable. Was he hurt?

A shout from behind had his head swiveling, and then his shoulders followed.

"Watch out man!" A bicyclist rode past, and suddenly Holden was down.

I ran.

"Fucking tourist!" he yelled.

I would have yelled the same. Locals knew better than to ride their bikes on the sidewalk.

I couldn't tell if he was hurt. He was on his hip, his legs under him.

"Holden, are you alright?"

I reached for him, too eager to help in my panic. I put my hand on his arm.

"Let me help you."

He brushed me away. "Get off me."

With a grunt, he pushed off the ground and got his knees under him. He took a long moment holding his position, hands and knees on the ground, panting.

"How can I help? Should I call an ambulance?"

He shook his head. "I fell, it's not an emergency. If you want to call someone, call the cops and report that idiot on the bike."

I got the distinct impression that my presence wasn't helping, even though that's all I wanted to do.

Holden hissed in and shifted so that he had one foot on the ground. His hands braced against that knee. He took several heavy deep breaths, and then held one and with effort and a groan, pushed himself upright. Once on his feet, he wobbled. He clamped a hand on my shoulder. I braced my knees to take his weight and put my hands on his waist to steady him.

He didn't use me as support for long. We stood there on the sidewalk holding onto each other for stability.

When he let go of me, I noticed his sleeve had gotten pushed up. I saw an angry red scar running down the length of exposed arm, stopping at his wrist. What other scars was he hiding? His face was red from exertion and sweat dotted his brow. His mouth was pinched tight as if he was holding something in. His khakis had a tear at the knee, and I was fairly certain I saw blood. He wasn't in good shape.

"Come inside Holden, you can sit and rest for a bit. Let me help you get cleaned up."

"I don't need to rest. I've got this." He bit the words out.

"But you're—"

"I'm fine," he cut me off. "I don't need your help, and I sure as hell don't need your pity."

I stepped back as if he had pointed a flamethrower at me. Blinking hard with confusion, I stared at him. "Holden?"

He glowered at me. I had a sinking feeling in my stomach. Coming out here to help him had been the wrong choice.

"Where were you when I actually needed you? I don't need you running to my side, Makenzie. Not now, not ever."

"You are making no sense. You wanted me to wait and see if you were seriously hurt?"

"You didn't wait for me. So, I don't need your help now, okay? Maybe you should listen to your big brother and stay away from me."

I backed away from his verbal attack. I wanted to say something, but words lodged in my throat. I didn't understand what Travis had to do with any of it.

"Go away, Makenzie. Pretend you don't even know me if you see me again."

With stiff movements, he started walking away from me. I was stunned in place. What had just happened? I had run outside to help him up, but it felt like he was reacting to something else.

Was he angry that I had stopped writing him letters all those years ago? That didn't seem particularly fair since he had never bothered to write to me.

It was clear he was no longer the man I had been in love with, but I didn't see why after all this time we couldn't at least be civil to each other.

I threw my hands up. Fine, he didn't need me. I had made it this far without him, I could keep going on as we were.

I stormed back into the shop. He could fall down on the sidewalk again for all I cared. I wouldn't be there to scrape him up next time. I rushed to the bathroom in the back and slammed the door. I wasn't ready to tell Gloria what had happened, and I knew she would have questions. Hell, I had questions.

14

HOLDEN

Guilt ate around the edges of my pain. I had lashed out at Makenzie, the one person who actually had wanted to help me.

That fall hurt a lot. And it had opened old wounds I would have sworn were sealed over with scar tissue.

She didn't deserve to be treated like that.

I was always saying her brother was an asshole when the truth was. I was one too. And maybe even a bigger one, because I had lashed out on purpose.

I made it back to my car and sat for a while before I asked to be taken home. The pain had zapped me of my strength in ways that no one had prepared me for.

Instead of lashing out at the thoughtless tourist who had nearly crashed into me, throwing me off my balance, I yelled at Makenzie.

The words streaming out of my mouth had relieved some of my frustration, but the look on Makenzie's face had not been worth it. But instead of taking everything back as soon as I uttered the words, I doubled down and made everything worse.

I hit my head on the back of the car seat. I was such a fucking asshole. It wasn't her fault she had moved on, and I hadn't. At home, I leaned heavily on the cane to help me limp into the house.

I hated to rely on pain medication this far into recovery, but the spill after that asshole on the bike practically ran me over had me thinking about taking something stronger than a few ibuprofens.

I chased the meds down with a cold soda. I no longer kept beer in the house, not after I accidentally washed a heavy-duty pain pill down with a beer. Nothing had gone wrong, but it could have so easily gone sideways. I could be a real idiot, like how I had been with Makenzie this afternoon.

She was still so beautiful. It hurt to remember how she felt in my arms.

I had been a complete dick to her. And she was just trying to help.

I closed my eyes and tried to focus. All I could see was her face, her little chin, and her big eyes. The Makenzie I saw in my vision was the one I had in my bed all those times, too many years ago. She always looked up at me with sparkling eyes and a slightly pouty mouth with lips swollen from my kisses and a flush on her cheeks. She was the vision I had when I closed my eyes and had good dreams.

I let out a heavy sigh and crushed my palms against my temples. Maybe moving on had been her only option. Maybe moving on was what I needed to do. I would always have my visions of Makenzie, and my memories of her. And I need to be content with that now that I knew I would never be able to have her again.

She lived on the island now. I wasn't going to be able to avoid her. Not unless I left the island, and I wasn't exactly in a position where I wanted to do that. What I needed to do was man up and accept that she was married and had a child.

I knew how to be an adult. I had been in and out of combat situations. I navigated danger and yet nothing felt quite as perilous as how I needed to navigate my future around Makenzie and her little family.

At no point had coming home gone the way I had ever pictured it. Both of my parents were supposed to be alive. Makenzie would have waited for me, and we would have had a tearful yet sexy hot reunion. That's not what happened at all.

Why did I ever think that my life would allow me to come back and have everything stay the same?

I let myself drift off to sleep. My body needed the rest. I needed to heal. My heart might never recover, but there was no reason why my leg and arm couldn't.

I woke up the next morning, still in the recliner I had fallen asleep in. I was sore and stiff, but everything felt about a thousand times better.

I got to my feet and limped up to my room. I put on running shorts and the compression socks that helped to hide the worst of my scars. Breakfast was a power bar and another few ibuprofen tablets.

In my head I was about to hit the beach and go for a run. What really happened probably looked a lot more like a drunken stumble to anyone watching as I hobbled along with my cane. I probably wasn't supposed to be doing this but fuck it. If I didn't power through, how else was I supposed to improve?

Back at the house, I had an old set of weights. I knocked the worst of the dust off and got to work. I had lost so much strength in my hand and arm. I did a few reps with my good arm just to prove that I could. I could barely wrap my left hand around the handle of the weight, there was no way I could rotate my arm into proper form with my palm facing up as I would need to work on bicep curls.

With a scream, I dropped the weight.

Working out had always been my primary method of blowing off my frustration and thinking through problems. Running, weights, had all been ways of getting the clarity I needed. That wasn't happening today, or any time soon.

After taking a shower I changed into the long pants and long sleeves I had started wearing to cover the big red scars down my lower leg, and on both sides of my left arm. Under those scars were the pins holding me together.

I sucked in my breath as I limped into Dad's old office. I didn't exactly know where to start first. This room held years of business deals and wealth management. He had taken over his father's business, made some important changes, and taken the business in a very lucrative yet highly specialized direction.

My memories of this room were limited to my father always sitting behind the impressive mahogany desk that now faced me down and dared me to rifle through its drawers.

I wasn't going to be intimidated by a hunk of wood. I sat at the desk and took a moment. From this perspective, I saw what my dad had seen. There was no profound insight, I didn't suddenly understand business concepts. I wasn't mystically channeling my father letting me know what drawers could be cleaned out, and shredded, and what paperwork should be shipped off to the lawyers.

I opened and closed drawers, still no hint of what I should or shouldn't be doing.

The phone rang. I stared at the old handheld phone that sat on Dad's desk. There was no caller ID, no fancy buttons.

"Hello"

"Holden Wells?"

"Yeah, how can I help you?"

"My name is Penny Smith. I'm calling from the legal department at corporate."

The call couldn't have been timelier had I scheduled an appointment.

"I've been tasked with reaching out to discover what your plans were for stepping into your father's position?"

"About that," I let out a heavy breath. I was not in a position currently to step into my father's shoes. "I'm still in recovery. The board is managing perfectly well without me. I'm confident they will continue to do so. I need to ask you a question. Not sure if I need to speak with you, or if you need to pass me along."

"I'll do my best. What do you need?"

I explained my situation. I was in an office full of records, and I wasn't familiar enough with any of it to safely and legally make the call about what needed to be saved.

"I can definitely help with that. I will arrange to have some banker boxes shipped to you. If you could box everything up, and let me know when you're ready, I'll have a courier arranged to pick them up."

I felt a sense of relief when I got off the phone. A major weight was off my shoulders. Dad's paperwork was handled. There was still plenty to go through in his office. The shelves behind his desk were covered in books and old trophies. I was going to need something to sort all of this stuff into. I took a break and headed into town. There had to be an office supply store on the island that sold boxes.

15

MAKENZIE

I held the ladder steady as Ethan adjusted the sign. Gloria stood to one side and directed Ethan.

"Up a little more on the left."

Ethan moved the sign.

"Now back down a little," she directed. "Only like a quarter of an inch, okay."

"Mom, it's level. Are people really going to notice a quarter of an inch?"

"I will."

It was thrilling and nerves danced in my stomach. We were putting up the big sign. The sign that announced to the world we were a quilt shop. It suddenly felt like we had a legitimate business. We now had more than just a paper sign on the door.

People would now know what we were doing. I was going to have to draw up another sign for the door, announcing how soon we would be opening. Another two weeks was our goal. And we were on target.

I heard Ainsley crying from inside the store. I glanced up at Ethan, and back at the door.

"Ainsley's awake," I announced.

"I can't do anything about that right now," Ethan quipped from up on the ladder.

"I'm aware of that. I don't think it would be a good idea for me to let go and go get her."

"She'll be fine for a minute."

"You let my child cry?"

"You don't?

"I've got her," Gloria said. She sounded completely exasperated with us. "Just make sure that sign is straight before you screw it in."

"Thanks." I continued to hold the ladder steady while Ethan started drilling the sign into place.

"How does it look?" he asked.

"I can't exactly see it from this angle."

"Step back, tell me what you think."

"I shouldn't let go of the ladder with you still on it. That's not safe, and I would hate myself if you fall."

"Maybe I can help?"

I sucked in a quick breath at Holden's voice. He stepped in close, and the nerves that were already dancing along my spine went into overdrive.

"I'll hold the ladder; you go take a look."

His arm reached across me and grabbed onto the ladder.

"Are you sure? I mean, you've been hurt."

Holden laughed at me. "I only hurt one arm. I'm strong enough to keep a ladder steady."

"Okay." I nodded.

I let Holden take over, and I stepped to the far side of the sidewalk. Our quilt shop had a sign. Tears welled up in my eyes. I covered my mouth with my hands. My cheeks started to hurt and I smiled so hard.

I couldn't believe this was actually happening. It felt more real with the sign up than it had unpacking boxes of fabric. That had felt like playtime in comparison to this.

"It's beautiful," I yelled up to Ethan.

"Is it safe to come down?"

"It looks good," Holden added.

Ethan started to climb down the ladder. Holden stepped out of the way.

"Thanks," Ethan said.

Holden held out his hand. "Holden Wells, good to meet you."

"Ethan."

Ethan looked at me and back up at the sign. "If we're done, I'll put this back, and then I'll go check on Ainsley." He started to pull down the telescoping ladder.

"We're done. Thanks," I said.

I was tempted to follow Ethan inside, after all Holden had been completely ugly to me the last time, I saw him. "I should get going."

"Wait." He put a hand on my arm.

My gaze went to his hand, and I followed it up to his arm. He wasn't wearing a long-sleeved shirt, today he had one of those construction worker sleeves covering his arm. It was like a black tight sleeve that covered him from wrist up past his elbow. There was a small gap between the compression sleeve and his short shirt sleeve where I could see skin.

I met his gaze, and our eyes locked. The thrill of having the sign put up, and with Holden standing so close, my insides flipped with a completely different feeling. My pulse quickened, and I found it hard to catch my breath. I desperately wanted his arms around me.

"Ethan seems like a good guy." Holden's attention was on the new sign.

"He's great. I wouldn't be able to do this without him." He was a super handyman and a super nanny all rolled into one. Ainsley certainly adored him. She was going to miss him when he headed back to school in the fall. I knew I was too.

"How did you meet him?"

"He's Gloria's son. She's my business partner and mom's friend. We're all kind of interconnected. Sort of like how we used to be. My parents, your parents, my brother." I paused. "Us."

"Makenzie, the ladder provided me with an excuse to come over and say something. I need to explain my actions the other day," Holden started, cutting me off.

The way he talked fast made me think he had been waiting to say something difficult and now was his perfect opportunity. If he didn't get it out now, he might not ever.

"No, no. You were in a lot of pain. I could tell." I didn't want Holden to think talking to me was some kind of chore.

"Yeah, a lot of pain. I'm still pissed about that cyclist. I didn't handle it well, and I said things to you that I shouldn't have."

I bobbed my head in a noncommittal nod. I wasn't sure if he was looking for absolution or not. I really wasn't ready to give any. He had hurt my feelings four years ago, and all those feelings had come sneaking back in the dark when I couldn't sleep. His words the other day had brought up all those memories of hurt and loss.

I gave him a weak grin.

"So, a quilt shop, huh?" If I didn't know any better, I would have said Holden was reaching for something to talk about.

"Yeah, we will open in a couple of weeks. Look, I should probably let you go."

Even if Holden hadn't completely meant what he said when he told me to pretend, I didn't know him, part of me felt that he had said that for a reason. He was like a beautiful and dangerous animal, like a little poisonous tree frog. Getting too close was not a good idea. Touching was positively deadly. I would only get hurt. He had hurt me once; I was wary about being hurt again.

Holden released his grip on me, and the lack of touch was even worse than I could have imagined. It was a reminder of losing him. I had a sudden feeling that he would never touch me again.

"Do you have time to go get a coffee? Catch up on old times? I have missed so much. I want to know how you went from wanting to be an interior decorator to running a quilt shop with some friend of your mother."

"It's a long story."

"I have time," he said.

Well, I didn't. I had a shipment of fabric to unload and put on display. I still had to finish assembling the frame for the long-arm machine, and I needed Ethan to help me with that. I had grossly underestimated the amount of time that Ethan would be spending watching Ainsley. He was a great helper, but he spent his time unequally divided between Ainsley and helping set up shop, with the bulk of it watching my daughter. He was costing me a fortune, but he was worth it.

"Unfortunately, I don't have time right now. But I really would love to catch up. Maybe another time?"

Holden looked upset. Part of me wanted to take back my words immediately. I didn't want there to be more hurt between us. I probably had time for a stroll down the street, but not enough to really spend time talking with him the way we both needed.

He shrugged. "Yeah, sure. I'll let you get back to Ethan and your little shop," he said with bitter tones in his voice. "I won't bother you any longer."

I watched him walk away. He moved stiffly and the limp I had noticed the other day seemed even more pronounced. Was that because of the accident with the bike? Or was he hiding more than just scars with his clothes?

What kind of coming home reception had he gotten? He had come home, wrapped in bandages, and attended his father's funeral. What kind of a friend was I? I hadn't been able to say anything to him when he probably needed a friend the most.

I cast my gaze into the shop, and then back down the street to watch Holden's retreating form. Running after Holden seemed like something I would do if this were a movie.

"If it starts raining in the next thirty seconds, I will go after him."

I looked up at the perfectly clear sky. I didn't think I was going to get my movie moment of running after my lost love and kissing him in the rain. With a deep sigh, I headed into the shop. Unlike that movie moment, I knew how to use a phone, and I could still remember his phone number.

16

HOLDEN

I couldn't get Makenzie out of my head. She had been distant and aloof. I guess that was because she was married. Or maybe telling her to pretend she didn't know who I was had something to do with it. Either way, it sucked.

She hadn't seemed to want to spend any time with me. In all fairness, I didn't blame her. She was a busy business owner, and I was her past. She didn't need me in the way.

Only, I didn't want to be her past. I had always thought she would be my future and I wanted her. I had some half-assed fantasy about sweeping her off her feet and carrying her away from her family. She would forget about her husband and fall back in love with me. It was as much of a fantasy as those dreams I had where I woke up and I was whole, back on duty, and my dad was back in Connecticut with my mother, alive and well.

Neither was going to happen. They were as fantastical as dragons and wizards.

Makenzie seemed to actually like her husband. Somehow that made it worse, plus he seemed like a nice guy. So there went a change in my hypothetical plans of seducing her away from him. Not that Makenzie would ever allow me to do that.

She was kind and loyal. All the reasons I had fallen in love with her, were the exact reasons I would never be able to seduce her now that she was a married woman. She wouldn't look twice at me; her affections were focused somewhere else. And to be honest with myself, did I really want a woman who could so easily be lured away from her husband?

I shook my head; my thoughts were crazy-making and stupid. I wouldn't seduce a woman away from her husband. Not even Makenzie, who I wanted more than I wanted oxygen. I wasn't that kind of man. I had to accept that whatever there had been between us had ended.

I needed to clear my head and think. A good hard run followed by a brutal powerlifting session would normally have me thinking straight. But my leg still wasn't strong enough to go out for a run, and my focus was shot. Everything seemed to make me think about Makenzie. I went into the rec room and stared at the weight bench. If I could sweat out all of my concerns and clear my head, I knew I would feel better. Using it was all just wishful thinking, I was too weak to even lift the smallest weight. But I forced myself to try. I could barely be able to curl my hand around the handle of a small weight, forget about holding on properly.

"Fuck."

I gave up and ran my right hand over my throbbing forearm, cradling it to my stomach. A new-born baby had more muscle tone than I did. I hated being this helpless. I hated the way my bones ached. Maybe today was one of the painkiller days. I could take a pill and drift off to sleep. I wouldn't exactly feel better when I woke up, but the deep ache where I could feel every screw, every pin, and my muscles sliding over the plates in my limbs would be gone. Recovery was taking too damned long.

The house phone rang. I wasn't going to get to it fast enough, so I decided to let it go to voicemail, and then I remembered that my parents didn't do answering machines. If something was important enough, they made sure the person calling would have their cell number. I was honestly surprised the house phone still worked. The phone kept ringing.

With a tired groan, I got to my feet.

"I hear ya, keep ringing." I limped into Dad's old office and picked up the phone.

"Hello?"

"I can't believe your old phone number works!" There was no mistaking Makenzie's sweet voice.

"Hi, Makenzie. What can I do for you?"

"It's more like what can I do for you. Are you still interested in catching up?"

Hearing her was better than any pain reliever I could take. Tension left my body, and I felt relaxed for the first time in hours.

"Yeah, sure. You want to meet up for coffee?"

I started remembering all the spots we would meet up that could have been totally random had anyone in her family, or mine, seen us. We spent a lot of time deep in tourist areas, knowing our families would avoid those. We didn't need to do that anymore.

"Not exactly. I was thinking a little more than that. Would you be interested in dinner?"

"Dinner, sure? When? Where?" I could think of more than a dozen little restaurants where we could meet and sit around for hours talking. Low light, fine dining, a glass of wine, and a beautiful woman.

I shook my head to get rid of that particular image. I didn't need to imagine Makenzie smiling at me across a candle-lit table, a soft smile on her lips, a plunging neckline exposing her sexy cleavage.

"My house. You remember where, right?"

Her house. I breathed in. Her house, where she lived with her family, her husband and her child, possibly even her mother-in-law.

"Of course, I remember where you live. I've spent more summers on this island and in that house than I've been away. I mean, I know I got hit on the head, and all but... You know, dinner sounds great." I definitely remembered where she lived. I drove past her house almost every night like some love-sick teenager driving past the house of my crush hoping to see her through the window. And every time I did, I felt like a fool and hoped that her husband didn't notice.

"That's fabulous. I realized it's past due. I should have invited you over as soon as I knew you were back home. But what's a little time between friends? We're still friends, right?"

She hadn't invited me right away because I had shown up and had been a complete dick to her. I hadn't behaved the way a friend would. I acted like a jilted lover. Maybe that's what I was, but I knew I was better than that. Makenzie deserved better than that.

"I will always be your friend, Makenzie, as long as you'll have me." I could do that. I could be her friend. She was the kind of person, even if only as a platonic friend, I needed in my life.

After being injured, and with Dad's funeral, the number of people who I thought I could count on as friends radically diminished. My life had become so compartmentalized. I had very few college friends left, but they didn't interact much with me once I joined the Army. I had Army friends that seemed to turn to dust as soon as I was out. Friendship was a scarce commodity that I could use. Makenzie was offering an olive branch, I liked to think that I was smart enough to accept it.

There was a long silence on the other end of the line. It was too easy to imagine that she was smiling and blushing. She was probably simply conferring with her husband over something. I had to remember she was married. And that meant off-limits.

Getting to know her again as an adult and getting to know her husband might be exactly what I needed in order to get over her. Maybe I wouldn't be so completely attracted to Makenzie, who is now someone's wife and also a mother. I doubted it, but I needed to try.

"We can have a little coming home celebration."

"That sounds nice, Makenzie. I'd like that." I would like that entirely too much.

I leaned back in my father's desk chair and propped my feet on the desk in front of me. I enjoyed listening to her voice.

"What did you have in mind?" I asked.

"How does Monday evening sound?"

I stared up at the ceiling and thought about it. Something about Monday tickled the back of my brain. I didn't have any appointments. As far as I knew my schedule was completely empty. "Monday? I think I can clear my schedule. I'll show up around six?"

"Sounds like a plan. I'll see you then." She ended the call.

I swear I heard her giggle as she hung up. It was going to be tough convincing myself that she wasn't attractive. A small intimate family dinner was going to be good for my soul.

I swung out of the chair and limped off to the kitchen. I looked at the calendar hanging on the refrigerator. Dinner with Makenzie and her family on Monday. I was going to need to pick up a bottle of wine.

I kept my finger on the date and ran it back and forth between the box for Sunday and the box for Monday. No wonder Monday was tickling my brain. I closed my eyes and shook my head. If Makenzie entertained the way her mother used to, this wasn't going to be a small family dinner. This was the annual start of the season kick-off party. There would be a house full of people in for the season.

I didn't need to get wine, I needed beer. Monday was Memorial Day.

17

MAKENZIE

"Thank you for taking Ainsley with you," I thanked Gloria again for the thousandth time as I helped to install Ainsley's car seat into the back of Gloria's car. "I can't believe I totally forgot it was Memorial Day."

"How did you forget that?"

"Because it's May, and all my focus for the past two months has been on June twelfth, when we open the store."

"Your mother used to host the biggest start of the summer parties."

"I know. She was a little disappointed that I wasn't doing one this year. Seeing how it's her tradition. But I just don't have time, not with the store."

I picked up Ainsley who patiently stood, holding Gloria's hand. "You better be good for Ethan's mommy, okay?"

"I wanna play Ethan," she said, not quite whining.

"I know you do, baby, but he's off doing big boy things. He'll be back to play with you tomorrow. Can you be good?"

She nodded and gave me a slobbery kiss on the cheek. I kissed her right back. She was still little enough that I received baby kisses, but big enough to understand that going off with a babysitter wasn't the end of her world.

We had suffered from separation anxiety when she was much smaller, both of us. As soon as I finished school, and graduated, I put an end to having a nanny take care of her. I was fortunate enough that my parents were willing to continue to support me, emotionally and financially so that I could be with Ainsley as much as possible. Their encouragement and care allowed for my quilting obsession to take off. What had started as something I could do while still being with Ainsley quickly turned into a small business, selling my unique designs. But we were both better now. And I still planned on having her with me at the shop.

I buckled Ainsley in and was about to thank Gloria, again.

"What time should we head back? I don't want to interrupt anything." She wiggled her eyebrows at me conspiratorially.

"It's not like that. We're just old friends. Is eight too late?"

"I'll text you when we're headed back, and I'll shoot for eight."

"That sounds like a plan." I leaned into the back and gave Ainsley another kiss and watched as Gloria backed out of the driveway.

I let out a big breath. This wasn't a date. This was Holden coming over so we could talk, catch up. It was no different than picking things up with Nantucket friends at the beginning of the season after wintering off-island. That was it exactly.

So why was I so nervous? Why was I worried about how my makeup looked, and if this dress was showing too much boob or not? And if this was a date, was I showing enough cleavage?

Not a date.

I was in the kitchen when Holden walked in the backdoor.

"Where is everyone?"

"Everyone who?" I asked as I pulled the casserole dish from the oven.

"When I realized you invited me over on Memorial Day, I figured you were hosting the big start of the summer party."

I let out a bitter laugh. That explained why he came strolling in through the back carrying a six-pack of beer. On party days it was proper form to just come on in.

"I'm sorry about that. I completely spaced on the fact that it was Memorial Day until yesterday when I was at the grocery store. No party this year. Maybe next year after things have settled down."

"That smells good. At least you're still feeding me. And beer goes with Mexican, so it isn't the social faux pas it could have been."

I smiled. No, the social faux pas would have been on my behalf if I hadn't forced myself to stop worrying about how I looked and pulled my hair back into a ponytail. Holden clearly understood this was not a date. He wore plaid shorts and a polo. He almost looked like a golf pro on vacation, except for the black compression sleeve he wore over his left arm and the ace bandage that wound up his left leg.

"If you want to grab some glasses, you remember which cupboard? We're all set for dinner."

I carried the casserole dish over to the table that was mostly ready for us.

"Only two place settings? Where's Ethan?"

"Oh, he's got the day off."

"You gave your husband the day off?"

"What? Ethan, my husband? Oh, God no." Laughter bubbled up. I didn't know what was funnier, the idea of Ethan and me in a relationship, or that Holden had thought that.

"Ethan is my nanny."

"I thought he was your business partner's son." Holden looked confused.

"Well, yes, that too. He's been helping out around the shop and needed another job to carry him through the summer. I still haven't completely settled into living here, and I haven't had time to find and hire a nanny." I lifted my shoulder in a half shrug.

"So, he's not your daughter's father?"

I closed my eyes and bit the inside of my cheek. I knew this was coming, I hadn't expected it to be how we started the evening.

"How are the enchiladas? They aren't too hot, are they?" I attempted to redirect the conversation.

"They're great. I didn't know you could cook."

The nerves in my stomach rioted. The thought of putting food on top of the chaos inside felt like a very bad idea.

"Things have changed in the past few years. I cook, I sew."

"You own a small business."

"I do. Some days I can hardly believe it. And other days I'm drowning in it."

"And your business partner and her son are helping you figure it all out?"

"They are."

He leaned in close. "Okay, so if Ethan isn't your husband, how old is he? Because I've been struggling, trying to work out if he's just really young looking or if you married a younger man."

This time when I laughed the built-up stress left my body.

"I think he's nineteen. Maybe twenty. He just finished his freshman year."

Holden shook his head. "A male nanny? I can't believe I thought he was your husband. What does your husband think about you having a younger man watch your daughter?"

"Her name is Ainsley, and I'm not married."

"Not married? That certainly changes everything," he said with a sigh. The grin that spread over his face turned my insides to mush. I hadn't expected having dinner with Holden to be such an emotional roller coaster. I should have. I was still very much attracted to him. And possibly even a little in love with him still.

"No." I shook my head. "Everything is exactly the same, well at least for me. That's crazy that you thought of Ethan and me?" I did an exaggerated shiver. "I wouldn't even want to date him. He's a good guy, but... no."

"So, you're single? Not seeing anyone?"

I confirmed, "Single, not seeing anyone. I don't have time. Plus, I'm fairly picky. You set a high standard, Holden."

I didn't look at him and ate a few bites of my food. When I looked back up, he was staring at me, his lids were lowered, and his lips pulled up ever so slightly. It was more of a smolder than what I was prepared for. I felt it in my core and all the way to my toes.

"I want to see you, Makenzie."

"You're looking at me right now," I pretended to not understand his intentions.

"You know what I mean. Is it possible for us to find our way back to what we had? Date me, let's find out."

I sat back and worried at my lip. "I don't know Holden. A lot has changed. Emotionally I don't know if I could go back." And I didn't. I had been hurt; I didn't know if I could handle being hurt by him again. My body was reacting on a different level, its reaction was all yes, while my heart hesitated.

"I've got a kid. I'm starting a business. I don't know how dating fits into my life right now."

"Are you going to let me meet her, your daughter?"

I shook my head. "No. Not for a while."

"Why not?"

I didn't expect him to understand. Honestly, this was the first time I had to navigate this situation, even though I had thought about it. I had to protect her; I didn't want to confuse her by introducing men she might not ever see again.

"I don't introduce her to the men I'm seeing. Even though I know this isn't a date. But if we did…"

"You date a lot then? Do you, Makenzie?" Bitterness laced his words as if he was drinking it out of a bottle.

He glared at me before pushing to his feet.

"Would you introduce her to her father?"

I blinked hard. How had he figured it out? I hadn't said anything. He didn't even know how old she was. I swallowed hard and found my bravery.

"Are you assuming she's yours?"

"I know how to count, Makenzie. I can read between the lines." He sounded so incredibly smug.

"I didn't know you knew how to read at all. You certainly don't know how to write."

"What the hell is that supposed to mean?"

We were both yelling. I surged to my feet.

"Maybe if you had responded to any of my letters you would understand anything about me. I think you need to leave."

"You are a stubborn woman, Makenzie." He glowered at me and stormed away. The back door slammed shut.

I fell back into my chair and sobbed.

18

HOLDEN

I had to complete a few errands, so I arranged for a car to take me into town. I was too sore to give in to my personal vanity and not use the cane. After my first stop at the office supply store for more packing boxes, I had the driver head farther into town.

I started my daily prescribed walk at one end of the block. As a reward, I stopped in at the coffee shop. The last person I wanted to see was Makenzie. So, it made perfect sense that I kept running into her. She was there in the line in front of me. I had my cane with me, and for a second thought about ditching it somewhere so she wouldn't see it.

I didn't know why I was trying to impress her. She could see me for who I really was, a broken man needing tools to aid in my recovery. I stared at the back of her head and dared her to turn and look at me. I leaned on my cane and limped with exaggerated emphasis. Oh, look at me, I am an injured man.

Did I want her sympathy?

What was wrong with me? She had been pretty damned clear a few days earlier that we were very much in the past.

She was laughing and tossing her hair as she spoke to the young man behind the counter. Was she flirting with him?

I glared harder at her back. My gaze slid down the perfect curve of her back and I sucked in a breath. Her hips and ass were abundantly curvaceous and on display in a pair of tight jeans. I tightened my core muscles and grit my teeth together. Her body always sent mine into overdrive. My groin tightened as blood flow redirected itself. I may have been pissed off at her, but my dick was ready to stand at attention and say, 'yes ma'am whatever you want.'

Our eyes met, and she paused. She bit her lower lip. Her cheeks flushed, and she looked like she was about to say something.

Say anything, I should have begged right then.

Instead of saying something flirtatious, hell, I would have settled for a scathing retort, she raked her gaze over me from head to toe. When she brought her eyes back to meet mine, she narrowed her eyes into a glare and wrinkled up her nose as if she was smelling something bad.

She made it perfectly clear that she thought that me and my attitude were what stank. She walked past with a little huff.

Had I been whole, and able, I probably would have jumped out of line and ran after her. I wasn't in any condition to fight for her. Closing my eyes, I accepted my defeat and stayed in line.

With coffee in hand, I sat at a small cafe table and doctored my coffee to the way I liked it. I limped over to the trash can and reached out to toss my garbage at the same time as another person. I looked up and it was Makenzie. She pursed her lips and turned with a toss of her hair. The air filled with the soft scent of her coconut shampoo.

I got it; she was angry with me. I returned to my seat and made sure I watched as she walked away and up the street. She wiggled in the most delightful way when she was in a hurry. But more importantly, I had visual confirmation that she was well away and that I wouldn't run into her the next time I got up.

There was a small gift shop on this block that I wanted to visit. Mom always admired the little things the gift shop carried. I thought it would be a nice gesture to send her something to brighten her day. I walked slowly, careful to keep a good grip on both the cane and the coffee cup. The cup proved to be a bit tricky with my left hand, but I managed.

I set my coffee on the windowsill out front of the shop. It was a gamble that it would be there and untouched by the time I came out of the shop, but I wasn't willing to risk having a clumsy moment inside. Not with my grip strength being as weak as it was.

The shop bell tinkled and the clerk and the woman she was talking to turned to watch me hobble in.

"You again? Really?"

Makenzie's voice cut through the thoughts in my head. I completely forgot why I was there.

I must have stopped and stared for a moment.

"How can I help you, sir?" the shop clerk asked.

"Uh, I'm just looking for..." Why the fuck was I in there? Right, Mom. "For my mother."

Remembering took a moment longer than it should have, Makenzie had derailed me so completely.

"Let me know if you need any help."

I limped around the small shop. Instead of looking at trinkets and small items with positive sayings emblazoned across them, I kept casting my gaze to Makenzie.

She looked really good all grown up. She had always had good curves, but now they were even better. Being a mother had done amazing things for her shape. She looked like she would be soft to hold.

My left hand decided that was the perfect moment to fumble the small ring box I had picked up and pretended to be looking at.

"Sorry, sorry," I said, as I carefully replaced the box.

Makenzie leveled her glare at me. She obviously didn't believe for an instant that I was there for a random gift for my mother.

I needed to get out of there before Makenzie accused me of stalking her. It was a small island; she knew we would eventually run into each other.

"Thanks for coming in," the clerk called out as I limped from the store.

My coffee was where I had left it, untouched. It was cold. I tossed it in the first trash can I found. The island was full of little gift shops. I could find something in one of those. Fortunately, I didn't have to walk far before I found another shop.

The items were similar to the previous shop. I was bound to find something here. I walked slowly around the display tables letting my gaze fall on the various items on display.

I picked up a small painted figurine of a heart with flames coming off the top. I flipped it over and it had "Burning Love" incised into the bottom. It seemed like something Makenzie would like. A little folk-art style, a little edgy. I held onto it as I kept looking for something for Mom.

I was at the counter paying for a small box with inlaid turquoise and the Burning Love sculpture when the door opened, and I heard an exasperated sigh.

"Seriously Holden, what are you doing here?"

I huffed half a chuckle out through my nose. "I was here first. Tuck your attitude back in. You can't accuse me of following you around like a love-sick puppy. I had no idea you would be coming in here. As I said the last time I saw you, I'm buying a gift for my mother."

"Whatever for? Is it her birthday?"

"No, as you might recall, she recently lost her husband of thirty-five years. I thought I would send her something to cheer her up."

Makenzie rolled her eyes and shook her head at me.

"I'm almost finished. I'll be out of your hair in just a minute."

She stood with her arms crossed and watched as I limped past her and out the door. The situation was ridiculous, I couldn't help but smile.

With my purchases in hand, I headed back to where the car would be waiting for me. I slid into the back with a sense of relief. I had done a fair bit more walking than I had intended. Keeping my cool around Makenzie had taken more effort than I would have expected.

Damn, she was so beautiful. And she was single. It didn't matter that she had a kid, I still wanted her. I sat up. She had a kid. I started to count on my fingers. There was no way.

I leaned back into the car seat and closed my eyes. How old was her daughter? There was a very real possibility that the little girl was mine. Wow.

I began to rethink everything Makenzie had said about not introducing her kid to random dates. As some random guy in Makenzie's life, yes, I wanted to meet her daughter. I understood that single mothers came as package deal with children. But as the potential father of that child, I was very glad that Makenzie was as smart as she was and protecting our child.

19

MAKENZIE

Ainsley swung her legs and pointed at the grapes she wanted.

"These?" I asked, holding up the dark purple ones.

"The green ones," she corrected.

"I like the purple ones. How about we get both. What else do we need?"

"Bananas."

I pushed the cart through the produce section, letting her help decide what food she would eat for the week. Not that it helped her to eat new things, but I tried. Holding up a zucchini I asked, "Will you try this?"

She squished up her face and shook her head.

"Which one will you try?" I picked up a cauliflower next, and then some broccoli.

She gave me a reluctant nod for the broccoli.

"Okay, I need you to remember that you agreed to try broccoli when I make it for dinner."

She pouted in reply.

"Ainsley?"

"Try." She may have said other words but all I heard was an acknowledgment for trying.

I turned out of the produce section and stopped.

"Oh, you have got to be kidding me." Coming into the store behind a shopping cart was Holden.

Nantucket was a small place, but this was getting ridiculous. I couldn't get away from the man. There were people on this island I never saw, never ran into out shopping. Why couldn't he be one of them?

I moved in the opposite direction, keeping behind him, and just out of sight. I really did not want a repeat of the other day.

I had been out sharing our grand opening information and introducing myself to my new business neighbors and he was everywhere. I couldn't shake him.

"Time for us to skedaddle," I leaned in and whispered to Ainsley.

She giggled, thinking I was being funny.

I kept looking over my shoulder as we waited in the checkout line. So far Holden seemed to be on the far side of the grocery store, and out of sight. Out in the parking lot, I let my guard down. Holden was inside, I was safe. Or so I thought.

I got the groceries unloaded, and Ainsley secured in her car seat and was returning the cart to the in-lot coral when I heard his voice say my name.

My head snapped up, and there he was, standing in front of me.

"We can't avoid each other forever," he said. He shrugged his shoulders and gave me a half-smile.

Damn if my insides didn't go all gooey at the thought of an apology from him.

"I can try." At least my smart-ass attitude wasn't going soft simply because Holden Wells smoldered at me. Maybe I was fooling myself, but I was a firm believer in the fake-it-til-you-make-it philosophy, even if that meant pretending, I didn't melt into a puddle of nerves and want whenever he was near me.

"You aren't even willing to say 'hi?' Meet me halfway?"

I glanced over my shoulder at my minivan. I had the side door open, and Ainsley was complaining inside.

"My daughter is in the car. I can't hang around chit-chatting all day."

"You could introduce me."

I sighed. "I could." I should, considering everything, but I wasn't going to, not until I knew what firm ground with Holden looked like. "But I'm not going to. I explained it to you already. I don't introduce random people to her, I don't want her confused about the men in my life, or in hers."

I turned to go.

"Makenzie." His brow was furrowed, and he looked so concerned.

I closed my eyes against the surge of emotions I felt. I wanted to run to him and wrap him in my arms, tell him everything would be fine. But I couldn't. I had no way of knowing if once he recovered, he would leave me again.

I didn't want to live through that pain again. And I certainly wasn't going to introduce him to Ainsley, only to have her father vanish on her as well.

"I've got to go. I'll think about it."

I thought about it a lot when he first went away. How was I going to tell him that I was pregnant? I wrote him telling him I had big news, exciting news. I wrote to him and begged him to please write me back. I had something important to tell him. I wrote to him and eventually told him to never mind, I guess I was going to manage everything on my own. And I stopped writing, but I kept hoping. Eventually, that died in me as well.

I slid behind the wheel. And hit the button to slide the doors closed. "Please keep your arms and legs inside the ride at all times," I announced like an amusement park ride.

Ainsley didn't give me her usual giggle, she squirmed and made complaining sounds. She was getting hungry. I missed not having fast food available. The best I could do on the island was a drive-thru espresso shop that also had muffins.

As I navigated in that direction, I noticed a food truck set up in the parking lot of a hotel. I pulled in on the off chance they were open and had french fries. Parking next to the food truck, I opened the side door on my van so that I could see Ainsley, and she could see me. If they didn't have anything on the menu she would eat, I wouldn't have to wrestle her out of her car seat and back in again. Besides, I was only twenty feet away and could keep an eye on her.

"Can I help you?"

I read over the chalkboard menu and was pleased to see toddler-approved french fries and chicken nuggets.

"Yeah, french fries and chicken nuggets, please? You don't have juice boxes, do you?" I asked.

In my haste to escape the grocery store without Holden seeing me, I hadn't picked any juice boxes up. Maybe I could send Ethan out later.

"We have the pouches, but not boxes. Is that okay?"

"Yes," I nodded enthusiastically. And because I was in a bad habit of forgetting to feed myself when ordering Ainsley her lunch I added, "I'll also have a grilled fish sandwich and a Coke."

I paid for my order and walked back to Ainsley. "I got you some chicken nuggets, okay. Food will be ready soon." I sat on the floor of the van next to her feet and let her kick me in the back as we waited.

The young man in the food truck leaned out and yelled, "Chicken nuggets, fish sandwich."

"I'll be right back," I said to Ainsley.

It only took a few steps to the truck before I was back and sitting by her feet again. I pulled the french fries out of the bag first. "These are hot, let's give them a second."

I blew on the fries and pulled out the chicken nuggets. They were also hot, but Ainsley wasn't as concerned about them as she was about the fries. While I let things cool down, I punched the straw into the juice pouch and handed that up to her.

My Coke made a satisfactory pop and fizz sound as I opened it. Finally, the fries were not too hot for Ainsley to eat. I handed the bag up to her and she began eagerly munching on them. Unfortunately, her enthusiasm for food quickly waned, and after only one nugget she refused to eat any more.

"Come on, just one more?" If she didn't have at least two, even on a day like today where she was clearly not in an eating mood, she would be a complete tyrant after her nap.

We compromised, and she ate half of a second nugget.

"More for me," I declared and popped it in my mouth. She might not have been hungry, but I was. So, I wasn't complaining about wasting food when I was happy to have a few chicken nuggets after I had finished my sandwich.

I tossed the garbage from our lunch and drove the long way home, expecting that Ainsley would be asleep before I turned the corner.

She was completely out by the time I made it home. I left her sleeping in the car as I carried the groceries inside.

On my last trip a dark car pulled into my drive, blocking me in. Holden climbed out of the back.

I crossed my arms and glared as I watched him approach.

"What are you doing here?"

"I didn't run into you anywhere else, so I had to come to you," he said.

"Holden, this is stalking. It's one thing for us to be in the same place at the same time."

"Makenzie, please. I can't stop thinking about it. You have to let me meet her."

"I don't have to let you do anything in regard to my daughter. But if this means you will leave us alone, fine. She's asleep right now, and I'm not waking her up."

"Understandable." He nodded.

I turned, knowing he would follow me.

I stood next to the open minivan. Ainsley was limp and slumped in her car seat, completely asleep.

Holden stopped and just stared at her for a while.

"She's beautiful."

My heart clenched as I saw emotion cross his face. Did he know? There was no way he could have figured it out.

"She looks exactly like you."

"My clone, I've been told. I keep looking for any hints of her father in her face, but he's not there."

He wasn't there when he needed to be. But he was here now, and I didn't know what to do about him.

20

HOLDEN

I stopped for a coffee reward after walking up the block without my cane. The break also gave me sufficient time to regain enough strength to complete the walk back to the car.

Makenzie swept in like a fresh breeze. Instead of glaring at me, she actually gave me a small smile and a shrug.

"Okay, so I guess you aren't stalking me," she said as she stopped by the table where I sat.

"No, but it's good to see you. I'd like to see more of you."

She bit her lip and looked away. Was that a blush I caught on her cheeks? She started shaking her head.

"Come on, don't say no before I've even asked you out."

"Are you asking me out, Holden? Is that what's happening?"

"Go out with me Makenzie."

"I can't. The shop is opening in a few days. I'm swamped. I'll see you around."

She left and I was no less determined to get her to have dinner with me.

A few days later I found myself in a flower shop. I browsed the various displays. I didn't simply want to order a random bouquet to be delivered. Today was important, and the flowers needed to be full of deeper meaning.

Seeing Makenzie's daughter, really looking at her did not give me the confirmation I thought I would get. Babies so often look like their father, but Ainsley was a perfect mini replica of Makenzie. Same flaxen hair, the same bow of a mouth, and she probably had the same eyes.

The only way I would find out for certain if I was the child's father was to get on Makenzie's good side. And the only way I could think of doing that was to convince her to go out with me. I began a relentless campaign; my first step was flowers.

"Do you see anything you like?" The young lady behind the counter asked.

I shook my head. "Not really. I was hoping you might have some information on the hidden meaning of different flowers."

"You mean like red roses signifying true love while white roses mean regret?"

"That's exactly what I mean."

"I can help you put together something that conveys your message. What are you looking for?"

I almost didn't want to say anything. After all, the message was very personal. Of course, there was a very real chance that Makenzie wouldn't be aware of the hidden meaning.

"Well…" I described exactly what I needed the flowers for. "A good friend, who doesn't realize what she means to me, has achieved something to be proud of. I want flowers that, if she knows, will provide the hint that I would like there to be more between us."

The clerk smiled an ear-to-ear mischievous grin. "Friends to lovers, oh this one is my favorite. And we need to put in a smattering of success. What's the budget?"

"Whatever it takes," I chuckled.

At first, I tried to follow her around the shop, and she swooped through collecting flowers. Eventually, I gave up and found a stool to sit on while she made her selections.

When she was done, she presented a very charming display in a cut crystal vase.

"Those are quite beautiful. What does everything mean?"

"I tried to pack this full of meaning, even the greenery is symbolic. I have one red rose, classic true meaning. But then I included orange roses for desire. Now the carnations, the reds, are a little more desperate and longing than a red rose." As she described the meaning of each, she gently touched the flowers, so I knew what each was. "The purple basil is for good wishes. The dahlias symbolize positive change. I pulled in yellows and pinks here to tie the daisies. Visually you need a cohesive presentation, while still wanting to deliver your secret message."

I paid extra to have them delivered that afternoon. I wanted Makenzie to receive them on the opening day of her quilt shop.

I left knowing that my wishes would be carried out. I had my driver park the car a few storefronts down from the quilt shop so that I could watch for the flower delivery. I climbed from the back of the car and began my slow walk to the quilt shop as soon as I saw the delivery boy go inside with my flowers.

Makenzie was still reading the note by the time I entered the shop. She looked up at me and smiled. It was the smile of hers that always got me in the chest and had me catching my breath.

"You really shouldn't have. But they are lovely."

I looked at her, my brows raised. There had been more to that card than a simple congratulations on opening her store.

She sighed. It was a big sigh, and the movement strained the buttons on her shirt. They were already fighting the good fight keeping her ample breasts contained. But that sigh was almost the end of a few buttons.

"Holden."

I had been caught staring. I shifted my gaze to meet her eyes. "Well?"

She was shaking her head. "I told you, I don't have time."

That was a no. But it certainly sounded like a temporary no, not quite as definite as her earlier rejections had been.

"I'm still proud of you, you've done an amazing job here."

"Thank you." Her smile was sweet, and I held that picture in my mind as I made my way back out to the car.

Over the next few days, I formulated my plan. I was willing to play the long game to get Makenzie to go out with me. I could send flowers to her every day, but that would backfire on me if I overdid it. And I couldn't have Makenzie thinking that I was stalking her.

I needed to get her back in my life no matter what it took. I was in that coffee shop by 10 a.m. every single morning for the next week, just to make sure I was there when she came in for her morning break, usually around 10:30 a.m.

"I see you're becoming a regular," she said one morning after just over a week.

"They have good coffee and my favorite view."

"We're nowhere near the ocean."

"The ocean isn't my favorite view." I could not help but run my gaze over her. She looked better and better with each passing day.

The next day, she wasn't there. The shop was open, it was the middle of the week. I waited well over an hour before giving up. I pitched my cold coffee, and instead of turning back down the block, I made my way to her shop.

"Good morning," Gloria, her business partner, greeted me.

"Is Makenzie around?"

With a tip of her head, she indicated that I should head into the back.

"Makenzie—" I stopped abruptly as I encountered a room full of curious faces looking in my direction.

"Holden, what are you doing here?" She stood at the front of the room holding up what I assumed was a quilt sample, it was a colorful collection of fabric.

"I ah…" I closed my mouth. I was not about to ask her out in front of all those women. Then again, maybe that was a strategy I hadn't tried. "You didn't get coffee this morning, I thought I'd check and make sure everything was okay."

She gestured to her surroundings. "I have a class this morning, as you can see."

I pointed to the front of the shop. "Can I have a word?"

Makenzie excused herself, and I followed her out.

"What are you really doing here Holden?"

"I told you. I thought I'd check to make sure everything was all right when you didn't get your morning coffee."

"That's it?" Her shoulders bounced with quiet laughter.

"What's so funny?"

"You. You came to check on me, but not ask me out?"

"Why would I do that? You're only going to tell me no, that you are too busy with the shop, or that you don't have a babysitter. I can accept when I've been defeated. Unless, of course, you are going to say yes, this time?"

She sucked in air through her teeth and shook her head.

We were interrupted when one of her students stepped from the classroom.

"Honey, we can hear you in there, and I'm here to tell you, that life doesn't get any less busy. There is an entire room full of grannies in there willing to volunteer to babysit so you can go out with this nice young man. He came in here to check on you, even knowing that you weren't ready to go out with him." She patted Makenzie on the arm and then continued down the hall toward the back of the shop.

We looked at each other for a long moment before Makenzie dropped her gaze.

"What do you say? You've got your choice of babysitters." I gestured toward her classroom.

Makenzie rolled her eyes and shook her head. "Fine, I give in."

"I don't want you to give in, Makenzie. I want you to want to go out with me; it's not a punishment."

She held her hand out to me, and I wrapped my hand around hers. It was soft and warm.

"I've missed you," her voice was soft and quiet, almost a whisper. "I would love to go out with you."

21

MAKENZIE

I ran my fingers through my hair. I shouldn't have washed it. It was too limp. The deep body-forming curls weren't doing their job. I had wanted lush shampoo commercial hair, but not the part of the commercial where the hair was dripping wet.

I fluffed my hair and double-checked my makeup. On any normal day, I wore a minimal amount, enough so that I didn't look sickly, and that people could tell I had eyebrows and lashes. The fine blonde hairs tended to lighten in the summer, disappearing even further into my completion. Tonight, I had a little extra brow action, and I wore false lashes. I swiped an extra shimmer of gold across my lips, and added coral lipsticks, instead of my usual colorless lip balm.

A lot of work had gone into making my face look natural but enhanced. My effortless appearance was nothing but effort.

The push-up bra I wore cut into my shoulders a bit too much to be comfortable, but what they did for my breasts was worth it. If I was going to go out with Holden, I wanted him to regret every day he stayed away from me, every word he never wrote. I wanted him to look at me and have his brain go smooth, and his dick go hard.

The nerves I felt were less about having him accept me, but if I could succeed at reducing him to quivering gelatine. I wanted some form of power over him. He had pursued me into a corner, and I didn't think it had been fair asking me out and having my class gang up on me to encourage him.

Even though I hadn't lied. I wanted to reconnect; I just didn't want to get hurt again. I had kept his secret when he asked, no one ever knew, not even my best friend in school, that we were seeing each other. But he hadn't kept his end of the bargain, that after graduation, first his, and then mine, he would announce our engagement. When it was time for that, he ran away.

He may not have seen it that way, but that's how it felt. This time, I wasn't hiding anything. If he wanted me, he needed to be honest about it. The nerves in my stomach threatened to riot. I had my convictions. Now came the real test, could I stick to them?

"Hey, Mak, there's a fancy limo out front," Ethan yelled up the stairs.

I stepped out of my room and walked down the stairs. "Ethan, we don't yell from upstairs, or from other rooms. It's not polite, and it teaches little ears bad habits."

"Oh, sorry. But there's a limo out front. I think it's your date."

The doorbell rang.

"Grab that, will you?" I asked as I hurried to kiss Ainsley. "Be good for Ethan."

Ainsley gave me a hug that was like a vice grip and pressed her mouth to my cheek in a sloppy kiss.

I grabbed my purse for the evening and met the driver at the door.

He stepped out of my way and gestured for me to walk to the car. He got in front of me and opened the garden gate that separated the house from the street.

The back door on the limo was already open, and Holden sat there. His hands rested on a cane propped between his feet.

"I hope you don't mind. I wasn't feeling up to your front walk."

"Not at all," I said as I slipped into the limo and sat across from him. "The cobblestones can be hazardous when you don't have full control of your balance."

I cast my gaze around the limo, and over my shoulder at the raised divider blocking the driver from view.

"This is excessive." I pursed my lips and raised my brows. I didn't want him to think I was as impressed as I was. The last time I had been picked up in a limo was for my high school prom, and this had a very different mood about it.

"I wanted to make a good first impression. I still can't drive, and I wasn't going to pick you up in an Uber."

"I could have driven," I said.

"But then none of this would be a surprise."

"I hope what I'm wearing is acceptable."

Holden leaned forward and let out a throaty almost purr, almost growling. "Why are you sitting so far away?"

I lifted my brows and smirked. My plot to have him bewitched was well underway.

"I wouldn't want to appear all mussed when we get where we're going."

He sat back and looked smug. "You are a tease, Makenzie."

I laughed. "Says the man who picked me up in a limo. If I'm a tease you are trying to flaunt your money. So where are you taking me in all of this luxury, anyways?"

"It's exclusive." He continued to smolder at me until the car stopped. We were at the marina.

When he said exclusive, I thought he might have meant one of the more upscale restaurants on the island. I wasn't thinking about a dinner cruise. And I certainly wasn't thinking about a yacht when the limo driver turned into a speedboat driver and ferried us out.

"Holden?" I couldn't wrap my head around the boat we were approaching. It looked like a spaceship floating out in the surf. "I thought your father was in aviation, not in superyachts."

"It's a friend's," he said as he followed me out of the speedboat.

Holden moved slowly, but I did as well. The ship was incredibly stable, and I didn't have to worry about sea legs. I followed him into the ship and into one of the inner rooms. It was a lavishly appointed sitting room, with a dining table set in the center.

The champagne flutes were cut crystal, and the strawberries were dipped in chocolate.

"Holden, you really do know how to impress."

He was standing right behind me, and when I turned, he put his arms around me.

"Tell me if I'm moving too fast."

I pressed my entire length against his body and twisted my fingers into the hair at the back of his neck.

"This was kind of my plan, to begin with," I confessed.

"To seduce me? Funny, that was my plan as well. I've missed you, Makenzie."

His lips descended on mine, and I forgot about not getting mussed before dinner.

I leaned into the kiss, pressing against him, pulling him closer. We stumbled and half fell onto the couch. I couldn't stop touching him, running my hands over the smooth fabric of his dress shirt, feeling the muscles in his arms as he moved.

He slid to the floor, and I gasped and reached for him, thinking he had fallen. But when he shoved my knees apart and pushed up my skirt, I knew he was fully in command of his actions. I pressed my hands down my hips and fought Holden to pull my knees back together long enough to get my underwear off.

He scraped his teeth along my inner thigh. He dug fingers into my hips, kneading as he grabbed onto me and pulled my hips to the edge of the couch. I fell back and let my head roll to the side. My breath came faster the closer he got to my core.

His hot breath caressed my pussy, and then I felt his tongue. I whimpered as he delved into my folds and began sucking on my clit.

I laced my fingers into his hair and held his head to me. Lightning crashed through my body, all from the wicked power of his tongue. I hadn't had a man touch me at all, let alone like this since the last time I had been with him.

He pushed my leg up and hooked it over his shoulder. I couldn't think, not with him doing such magical things to me. I rocked my hips wanting to get closer. I gasped and felt like I would levitate off the couch when I felt him slide a finger into my depths.

Holden was a man on a mission. He added a second finger, and it was pure bliss. Pressure built in my core. Each stroke of finger, each lick of his tongue, and every sucking kiss against my clit mounted the intensity of our actions.

"Holden, I..." I don't know why I tried to speak. I couldn't form cohesive thoughts, forget about complete sentences.

I cried out and curled in on myself and clutched his head to me as waves of orgasmic spasms took over my body. Shudders racked my body to the point where I couldn't do much of anything. I was wrung out and limp. But Holden didn't relent. He continued to lick and suck every twitch out of me.

I whimpered as his fingers slid from me. He sat back and smoldered at me. Running his fingers over his mouth, he licked and then sucked his fingertips into his mouth.

I lay there trying to catch my breath. I pushed my hair out of my face and struggled to sit up. "What was that?"

"Now, that's what I call an appetizer. Ready for dinner?"

2 2

HOLDEN

Makenzie looked like a woman completely satisfied. I wasn't sure she was going to move from the couch. I half expected her to curl up on her side and demand a blanket so that she could take a nap.

With a moan that had my cock throbbing even harder, she stood with a stretch. She adjusted her skirt with a wiggle and then sashayed over to the table.

While her back was to me, I, not so effortlessly, clamored back onto the couch.

My attention was drawn back to her when the champagne cork popped, and Makenzie giggled. She sort of danced a bit as she poured champagne into the flutes, and bit into one of the strawberries. Dinner was going to be torture watching her mouth wrap around things that weren't me.

She staggered back toward me, drinks in hand.

"My legs don't seem to be working very well."

"Either do mine," I joked as I took the offered glass.

"You're still a smart ass."

"The preferred term is charming." I looked up at her as she stood over me, her thighs pressed against mine.

I reached out and set the flute on the side table before running my hands up her legs, touching her skin.

"I was thinking." She pressed my back with a single finger against my chest. She proceeded to crawl onto my lap, straddling my hips. "Of skipping dinner and going straight for dessert."

Her lips were cool from the chilled drink.

I took her glass and set it next to mine. Again, she pressed me back, smoothing her hands over my chest, around the muscles of my shoulders.

I reached up her skirt again and grabbed her hips. I watched her face as she focused on the buttons of my shirt. She hummed as she undressed me. I recognized the tune, but I couldn't place it. At that moment, I wouldn't have been able to identify the Star-Spangled Banner. I had Makenzie in my lap and that's all I had attention for.

"May I?" I removed my hands from her hips and reached for her top.

She shifted her gaze from my buttons to her chest. Her lips twisted to the side, and then she looked through her lashes up at me. With what seemed complicated twisting of her arms at the moment, she crossed her arms and grabbed the hem of her skirt and pulled everything over her head.

I was breathless as she tossed her dress to the side. Her bra was black and lacy, and probably matched the panties she had tossed to the side earlier. I was a lucky man.

"I think I'd be disappointed if you didn't," she sounded as breathless as I felt.

I cupped the side of her breasts, skimming my thumbs in circles over the shiny fabric until I felt the nubs of her nipples.

Makenzie tugged on my shirt, pulling the tails from my waistband. I shifted enough to let the fabric pull free without ripping, and at the same time I took advantage of the new position and wrapped my mouth over her nipple through the fabric of her bra.

She hissed and wrapped her arms around my head, holding me to her breast. She filled my mouth, and my hand as I palmed the other breast, tweaking the nipple between my fingers. She was warm and soft. Somehow, I had forgotten just how amazing it was to have Makenzie in my mouth, moaning under my fingers.

She didn't hold still. She writhed and moved, rocking her hips over mine in the most tantalizing cock tease. I could feel the heat rolling off her body. My cock strained at the fly of my pants. I wanted to strip down and continue making love to her, but this was her game now. I followed her lead and was happy to go where she took me.

"Holden." My name was a murmur on her lips.

She tugged at my hair until I tipped my head back. She wrapped her hands around my face and stared deep into my eyes. Did she see how beautiful she was in my eyes? Could she tell that I still felt the same way for her now as I had so many years ago? Her eyes sparkled in the low light, and her lips were plump from earlier kisses. Hers was the face I wanted to look into for the rest of my life.

I wrapped my hand around the back of her neck and brought her lips down to mine. She kissed with enthusiasm and passion. She was almost frantic the way she sucked on my tongue, with a pulsing rhythm that matched the timing of her rocking hips.

"I need you," she said, finally breaking the kiss.

"I'm right here baby, tell me what you need."

"Skin, I want to touch your skin."

I couldn't rip my shirt off fast enough to meet her demands. Once the dress shirt was gone, I still had to pull the tee over my head. Makenzie spread her hands out over my pecs and purred as her fingers tangled into my chest hair.

"I forgot how good your skin feels," her words were mere whispers of breath.

She traced her fingertips down my arms, hesitating when she got to my scars. Then her touch turned curious and tender. She lifted my arm to her lips and kissed the long red marks that ran up my arm on either side.

"I'm sorry this happened to you."

"Me too, me too." I eased my arm away from her, not wanting to derail our current focus. She could ask about scars and injuries later.

I unfastened my pants and pushed them down, out of the way.

Makenzie moaned appreciatively when she gazed down at my lap. She bit her lip and looked like a hungry tiger. She could devour me any time.

"Condom?"

"Wallet, back pocket."

Without leaving my lap, she bent over, picked up my pants, and began fishing for my wallet. She handed me the wallet. I pulled out the condom and tossed the wallet to the side.

"Will you?" I asked as I handed her the foil pack.

She ripped it open with her teeth and spit the wrapper away. Her tongue slipped between her lips as she focused on rolling the condom down my length. Between her touch on me, and the sheer sexiness of her expression, I wasn't going to last long.

We both let out long moans of relief when she positioned herself and sank down on me. Her depths welcomed me, and for a moment cradled me in soft pressure and warmth. She started grinding. I thrust against her, and that soft pressure turned into a sucking pulsing sensation.

We moved together in a way that stole my recollection of ever having touched her before. This all felt so new, so perfect. Makenzie's eyes went wide, and she dropped her jaw. She fought for air between whining moans. I dug my fingers into her hips and pulled her down against me with each thrust I made.

She stopped rocking as her orgasm took over. Her inner walls squeezed and released my cock in a frenzied pace I could no longer match, triggering my orgasm. We cried out as we came together, each hitting that high that our bodies had driven so hard to reach.

She fell limp against me. I eased out of her and held her in my arms. This was how we were meant to be. We gazed into each other's eyes for a long time. Neither wanting to break the spell and let reality back into our lives.

I kissed her on the forehead and let her slip onto the couch. "I'll be right back."

I had to take care of the condom and wasn't feeling particularly stable after that.

"Need help?"

"I've got it." I used every piece of furniture between where I started and where I was headed as a temporary brace. When I returned, Makenzie was eating another strawberry, her dress back on.

"I can't find my panties. Do you think your friend, or at least their cleaning crew will be scandalized when they find them?"

"I hope so." I sat in one of the dining chairs. "Should I call for dinner now?"

Makenzie nodded. "I could eat. Please tell me it isn't chicken nuggets and french fries." She picked up the forgotten champagne flutes and moved to the table to sit across from me.

"Sounds like a delicacy fit for a toddler. I'll keep that in mind when she joins us for dinner next time."

"She won't be joining us for a while, if at all. I told you, I don't want to confuse her by introducing her to the men I'm dating."

"Does that include her father?"

Makenzie blanched and then flushed. "Her father isn't in the picture."

"I wasn't, but I'm back. I'm not just a man you're dating, Makenzie. Who else knows I'm the father?"

"What makes you think you're her father?" Makenzie's voice got loud and shrill. I didn't believe her indignation.

"I figured it out."

"Well, you figured wrong. And if you want to be a father figure, you're going to have to earn my trust first."

"Isn't that what—"

"That wasn't about trust, Holden, and you know it. That was lust and some unfinished business between us. You walked away from me once, you have to prove that isn't going to happen again before I can trust my daughter with you, as the man I'm dating, or as a father. And that's not saying you are her father. You are assuming a lot right now."

She surged to her feet. "I think that I'll pass on dinner, and have your driver take me back now."

23

MAKENZIE

I didn't like how I had left things with Holden. I loved what we had together, and the night before had reminded me of what we could be. But it also reminded me that so much had changed between us. I leaned on the counter staring at the phone in my hands. The shop was empty and quiet. I had nothing to distract me from my thoughts.

He hadn't called or texted me yet this morning. I wasn't planning on sitting around pining away hoping he would text or call. Communication was a two-way street; I just didn't know what to say. I not so secretly hoped he was feeling the same way. Last night was amazing until it wasn't. We needed to work on why it fell apart. We belonged together, but we kept messing up.

"Sorry, I may have overreacted." I typed. My thumb hovered over the send button. Instead, I hit the back button, erasing the confession.

I tried several different messages, typing each one out and then hesitating before erasing the words. None seemed to fit what I was feeling exactly. I couldn't bring myself to text what I was really feeling. I was in love with him again. Not again, still.

"Can we talk?" I hit send. Anything I needed to say to him shouldn't be sent over in a text message. I needed to be able to look into his eyes so that I knew he understood what I was saying.

I wasn't sure if I was satisfied with my message and was still staring at my phone when the chimes over the door jingled. I looked up to see a massive bouquet of flowers coming into the store. The delivery boy was hidden behind them. There were so many.

"These are for Makenzie."

"That's me." I felt a zip of excitement as he placed the flowers on the counter.

"Someone is in the doghouse," he said as he handed me a card.

"What do you mean?" I couldn't take my eyes off the elaborate arrangement. It was a mass of white tulips interspersed with lily of the valley and red roses with a ring of blue hyacinths around the base.

I didn't tear into the card but looked up hoping for an explanation.

"Tulips and hyacinths, specifically blue ones, are 'forgive me' flowers. Jenna at the store is really good with fitting flowers to the message."

I laughed. "Flowers have meaning? I thought they were just pretty and so the gesture was the thing."

"Everyone knows flowers have meaning, like red roses on Valentines for love."

"Sure, but I thought that was just roses." I reached up and touched one of the delicate red petals. "Then what are roses with tulips?"

He shrugged. "Best guess would be something like 'I love you, forgive me.' I mean that's the kind of arrangement Jenna would totally do. She's really good at combining flowers for that deeper meaning, you know?"

"Oh wow," I stared at the flowers, and barely mumbled a 'thanks, bye' as the delivery boy left.

I peeled open the back of the envelope. The card had a cute but sad-faced puppy with the biggest eyes and the most pitiful expression on the front. It wasn't a simple card with a few lines of a note and Holden's signature, it was a whole letter.

Mea Culpa Makenzie. The fault for last night falls firmly on my shoulders. I got carried away by your beauty, by excitement.

I haven't been thinking much about my future beyond the next physical therapy appointment, when will I be able to walk? How soon before I run? I realize I haven't thought about the future for a very long time. All I've been doing is waiting for the next mission and never beyond that.

Being with you again has me thinking about what next year will be like, what we will have together in five, ten, twenty years from now. You told me exactly what your boundaries were, and I pushed you to the point of having to defend your beliefs. I commend you for cutting me off, for protecting our beautiful child.

Please give me another chance.

I sniffed and wiped at a tear. Stupid card had me all emotional. Holden figuring out Ainsley was his when no one else had, was a burning arrow in my heart. I was both overwhelmed with joy and filled with pain and fear.

I picked up my phone and dialed his number.

"I got your text, did the flowers arrive?" he asked as he picked up the call.

"They did, and they are beautiful, and Holden…" I held my breath for a long moment. "The delivery guy told me all about the deeper meaning of the flowers. You really went above and beyond."

"I'm glad you like the flowers."

"I like you, and I like that you are listening. What are you doing tonight? I can get Ethan to watch Ainsley."

He let out a disappointed groan. "I'm headed out to Connecticut for a few days. Something has come up regarding Dad's estate and Mom wants me there."

"Oh." It was my turn to be disappointed. "Can you have your driver swing by the shop so I can at least thank you in person?"

"I'm already on the plane. If I had known you were feeling the same, I would have come to see you. Look, as soon as I get back, we'll have dinner again."

"And this time actually feed me?" I leaned against the counter, my back to the door.

He laughed, and I could feel it in my toes. "Something not so exclusive, maybe De Lucas. If we're out in public, I'll behave."

"So, you'll be gentlemen if there are witnesses? And what happens when you get me home for a nightcap?"

"I'll behave better," his voice was a low throaty purr that sent shivers over my skin.

If he was going to keep talking to me like that, I would be happy with take-out and the back seat of his car.

"It's a date. I've got customers. Have a safe trip."

"I'll call you when I'm back."

"Holden," I paused. "Don't take too long, come home soon. I've missed you enough." I was a breath away from saying I loved him when the chimes above the door let me know someone had walked in. As much as I wanted to sit on the phone with him all day, I had a business to run and actual customers for the first time all day. "I've got to go, customers."

"I understand. Makenzie?"

"Yeah?"

"I'll miss you too."

I didn't stop the smile from spreading across my face when I ended the call. I turned to see who came in. "Let me know if there's anything I can help you with."

The smile and all the expressions dropped from my face. Travis stood on the opposite side of the counter from me, his arms folded, and a scowl on his face. That expression was permanent on my brother's face, leaving deep grooves in his forehead and around his lips.

"What are you doing here?"

"I think the real question is what are you doing?" He sneered. In an exaggerated motion, he craned his neck to look around the shop. "Where are all your customers?"

"At brunch, drinking mimosas," I quipped right back at him.

"You aren't making any money."

Right at that second, no I wasn't. For a shop that had only been open a few weeks, we weren't doing too badly. None of that was his business.

"Mom sent me to look in on you."

"If Mom is curious about my business, she can ask me herself. She did help with the setup while she was out last month. Will you be staying at the house?" I really hoped he would say no. The last thing I wanted or needed was Travis in my home. Even if technically it belonged to my parents, and he had a room there.

"I don't suppose you have my room ready." He sniffed and looked down his nose at me.

He walked around the shop, curling his lip at the fabrics that were on display. Every now and again he would reach out and rub a piece of fabric between his fingers.

"Why would I? I didn't know you were going to be here. As far as I know, your room is as ready as you left it."

He glanced over at me and continued his tour of the shop. "I expect there to be clean sheets on my bed. I'll be back after dinner."

He turned and started to walk as if he were going to leave.

"You can put your own sheets on the bed when you get there. I'm not your maid, and I don't have help staying at the house."

He stopped long enough to listen, and then he stormed out of the shop. I hoped he stormed all the way off the island. It may have been petty, but I wasn't going to jump just because he said so. And if he tried any of his power games with me, I wasn't above calling in Mom. After all, if he was telling the truth, she's the one who sent him here to begin with.

24

HOLDEN

I was used to my injuries throbbing when there was a change in the weather or if I overdid it. Typically, the pain was dull and pervasive. It wouldn't go away no matter what. It took time and some level of pain medication. When I stepped out of the shower at my mother's place and was hit with an unusual stabbing sensation, I mentally took note so I could follow up with my orthopaedist if it happened again.

Mom looked a little less bad for wear than the last time I had seen her when she joined me for breakfast. If you could call a mimosa breakfast.

"You should eat something," I said as I dug into my food. I had become used to eating a hasty yet filling breakfast in the Army. I now thoroughly enjoyed taking my time over my meals and eating a large breakfast. I focused on a protein-heavy breakfast to help my bones. I eyed her drink with judgement as I stirred a powdered calcium supplement into my own orange juice, no Champagne for me.

"I've been having this for breakfast much longer than you realize," Mom said, lifting her glass.

"I don't doubt it, but you also used to have yoghurt or a piece of toast."

"Fine," she huffed and reached out to my plate wiggling her fingers in a hand it over gesture.

I offered a piece of toast already slathered in apple butter. "Your liver will thank you."

"You're going to wish you had one of these after getting to the lawyers' office." She tipped her glass to me before taking a sip.

"I'll probably want something stronger," I chuckled.

"Bet, you're buying lunch if you so much as think you need a drink after what we're headed into."

"Do you really think it will be that bad?"

"Holden, your father died. Everything is that bad."

I was out of my chair and wrapping my arms around Mom for a hug. At some point, I grew taller than her and hugging her no longer felt like Mom was holding me, but I was holding her. She had always been a force of nature, when had she gotten so small?

She patted me and sniffed. "Sorry, I didn't mean to bring the mood down. Some days are better than others."

I didn't want to let go. I knew how rare my relationship with my parents was based on what my school friends had said about their parents. Whatever this thing was with the lawyers, I was there to take care of my mother.

"I'll be ready as soon as I finish breakfast. What time is the car?"

"We have time, the appointment is at ten."

Dark glasses hid most of her face, and she did not take them off once we reached the offices where we were to have our meeting. Lawyers from Dad's company—my company—and the lawyer who handled my parents' personal assets were all there.

I leaned over to Mom. "Looks like I'm buying lunch."

She laughed, the meeting hadn't even started, and I admitted defeat. It was good to see her smile, even if it was for a brief moment.

There was no obvious arrangement as to how people sat at the long conference table. No clarity on our team versus their team type of deal. It turned out there was only one team, all of them working for us against an impending tax audit. In the boxes of paperwork, I had cleared out of Dad's Nantucket home office, the lawyers found inconsistencies.

Apparently, there were a lot of very expensive inconsistencies.

"The books that were sent over from Powell's home office did not match the ledgers that we had," McHenry from the company's legal team started. "We reached out to Clay and Silverstein to see if they had information that we did not. Maybe Powell did not realize that certain assets needed to be included."

"We are still in the discovery process, gathering and locating all of Powell's assets," Clay said.

"Wouldn't Dad have had everything listed?"

"Only if your father had taken the time to have everything in one place. Your father died unexpectedly. He hadn't gathered everything into a nice clean list for his estate planning, something we do see with older or sickly clients. I expect that had your father been aware, that is something he would have done."

"So, what are you saying?" Mom asked.

"Possible tax fraud, or embezzlement, both, or a simple mistake. We don't have all of Powell's assets accounted for," Clay said as factually as he could. From the look on his face, I thought he was as shocked as the rest of us were.

"As you can see here," He was pointing at a spreadsheet.

"No, I don't see." Mom had taken her glasses off and stared at the same column of numbers that I was looking at.

"May I?" Penny, who had been so helpful weeks earlier, pulled up a chair next to my mother and began pointing to the exact figures McHenry wanted us to focus on.

"Right here, Mrs. Wells. This figure should actually match the figure at the bottom of this column, but it doesn't."

She looked at Mom until Mom nodded. "Go on."

"This number is what was reported on all of those tax documents."

"And the other one is substantially higher. Oh." Mom sat back in her chair and looked at everyone in the room. "So, you need to know where that money went."

She looked at me as panic dawned across her face.

"We haven't discovered any additional bank accounts. Are you aware if your husband had anything offshore?"

Mom started to laugh. It was the manic laughter of someone trying not to cry. "Powell didn't do anything farther offshore than go to Nantucket every summer. And yes, I'm very well aware that's not the same thing. I couldn't get him to go to the Caymans with me. I always had to go with a friend."

"What's the damage?" I asked. "Can they come after him if he's dead?"

"They can and will go after his assets."

"What if we take it to them? We offer a repayment plan and comply with any investigations they want to do. We can afford that."

"It's going to cost millions."

"It's going to cost a lot more if we don't comply," I countered.

We had lunch brought in and continued to work while we ate. So, in a way, I did pay for lunch.

"May I?" Penny reached to take my finished container. She was walking around collecting everyone's finished dishes and loose napkins left over from our meal.

I handed her the container. "Will you meet me in the hall when you're done?"

I stood with a wince. The stabbing in my leg was back.

"I'll be right back," I whispered to Mom before I left the conference room.

I propped myself against the wall out of sight of the conference room.

Penny followed a few moments later. "What can I help you with?"

"Can I trust you to be discreet?"

She twisted and pointed back toward the conference room. "If it's related, you really should be speaking with Clay or McHenry. I have the least amount of influence or seniority of anyone in that room."

I shook my head. "This has nothing to do with my father's questionable financial practices. This is extremely personal, and I'm impressed with how helpful you are proving yourself to be."

"As long as it's not criminal and has nothing to do with the situation in there, I'll do my best. Yes, I can be discreet."

"I recently found out that I have a child. I need to find out what I need to do to make sure she is taken care of, even if the mother and I aren't together. What are my legal rights? That kind of stuff."

"Oh, okay. I can definitely make inquiries for you. Do you have confirmation with a paternity test?"

"I don't need one." Ainsley was clearly mine, why would I bother?

"I'm going to recommend you get one since it sounds like this child is already a few years old."

I shrugged. "Fine. Why don't you head back? I'll be there in a minute."

With a slight nod, Penny turned and walked back toward the conference room.

I waited until she turned the corner before I pushed off the wall. The pain in my leg grew more intense with each step. Even with my cane, I was struggling. Chills overwhelmed my body, and I had to fight shivering with cold along with burning stabbing pain in my leg. The hall grew longer, and my vision tunneled, growing gray around the edges.

I don't know how long it took, but my mom rushed out of the conference room before I made it to the door.

"Holden?"

I collapsed against her.

"Oh God, you're burning up. Someone call an ambulance."

25

MAKENZIE

"What is this?" Travis asked as he stepped into the kitchen.

"What is what?" I looked around the room, nothing was out of place that I noticed.

"Where's breakfast?"

"Milk is in there, cereal in there." I pointed to the refrigerator and then the cupboard.

"I was expecting you to have something a little more prepared, and a lot less messy." He swiped scattered cereal O's from the table where Ainsley had tossed a handful of her breakfast earlier.

I shook my head. "I have no idea where you got that idea from. This is breakfast around here. If you want something fancier, you are welcome to cook something for yourself. Or you could always go to one of the many restaurants that serve breakfast."

"I'm here and I have expectations."

"No, Travis, you have delusions. I'm neither your cook nor your mother. I don't give a shit what you expect." I closed my mouth tight and cast a glance at Ainsley. Travis had me so mad I was cursing in front of little ears with a parrot mouth. "You're a grown man, feed yourself."

He huffed and looked like he was about to ask me if I knew who he was. Travis's level of self-importance only seemed to get worse with every passing year.

"I want to go over your books."

"That's nice." I used a tone that said, 'I heard but I'm ignoring your stupid request.'

"Makenzie." Travis tried to scold me.

Fool him. I didn't care what he thought. He wasn't in a position to scold me.

"Travis," I said right back at him.

"Your toddler is behaving better than you are."

"That's because she doesn't have an older brother to deal with. How long do I have to put up with you?"

"I'll leave this afternoon after I have a chance to look over your books."

"Yeah, you keep saying that like I'm going to just give in. I have a business partner and a business plan, and neither includes you. So, you can leave after breakfast."

"Mom specifically asked me—"

"Mom can talk to me directly if she is so concerned. Look, she doesn't understand my business or the craft industry as a whole. She honestly thinks I'm just making this up as I go along. I'm not. I'm following a tried and trusted formula used in the industry. If I was so mistaken, then why did Gloria jump in with such enthusiasm?'

"There was not even a single customer in your store the entire day."

"That's bull and you know it. There wasn't anyone in the while you were there. My business is doing just fine for having been open less than a month. Tell Mom that."

The alarm on my phone went off.

"Time for us to get ready to go," I said as I lifted Ainsley from her chair. I put her down and she ran off toward her room. "Don't be here when I get home. And next time you're planning on coming to Nantucket, call first, would you?"

"What? In case you don't have room for me? This isn't your house Makenzie."

I sighed. "No, but it's my home, and you don't have to be rude and just show up."

I cleaned up Ainsley's messy eating and tossed the dishes in the sink before following her upstairs. Travis was gone when we left about half an hour later. I hoped he stayed gone.

I spent the morning setting up a small, gated area that Ainsley could play in. She was happier when she could move around.

A couple of moms with toddlers in strollers came into the shop. Eavesdropping was inevitable, what with the size of the shop, and how loud they were. I had to keep my ears open in case they needed help.

"Oh, I'm going to have to come back. Look at all this gorgeous stuff."

"No sweetie, let's not touch that. That's not for you."

I was glad she was telling her kid to keep their grubby hands off my fabrics. Toddlers are adorable, but they are grubby.

"Excuse me?" One of them called out.

"Yes? How can I help you?"

She was standing in front of the play area I had set up. Ainsley sat playing with a couple of dolls.

"Is this for anyone? Or just..." She bit her lip and didn't finish asking.

"I hadn't thought of that. I was just giving my daughter a bit more playroom. You want to put your kids in there while you shop, why not?"

They both immediately began lifting their children out of their strollers. "Oh, thank you, this will make things so much easier."

Their kids found toys and began playing.

What I had anticipated as a quick fifteen-minute run through the shop turned into almost an hour's stay and several hundreds of dollars of yardage being sold. They happily chatted as they rolled their kids, back in the stroller, out the door.

Gloria held the door open and watched them leave. "Big sale?" she asked as she made her way back to the counter.

"Huge sale, all because of that." I pointed at the play area I had set up. "They were talking about having to come back later without their kids when they asked if they could put their kids in with Ainsley. I said sure, and they went nuts.'

"Well, when I was a kid, stores had playrooms so mothers could shop. I think they had to stop for liability issues."

I sighed; my brilliant idea had been squashed before I had a chance to verbalize it.

"But I think that was because they literally left us in rooms unattended and went all over in huge department and furniture stores. This place is small, they can see their kids from every single angle here."

"So, you're thinking what I'm thinking? We could move it a little farther back, and it could be seen from the classroom."

"We could offer mommy quilting days," Gloria said with excitement.

"We totally could. Moms are more tolerant of other kids than other people. So, we could offer classes specifically knowing that little kids will be present." I started laughing. "I was just thinking of asking Ethan to build us some low walls, making it permanent because of the sales. I hadn't even thought about class opportunities."

"We can expand classes to include toddler clothes."

"That's exactly what that one woman said she was going to make. She bought over three hundred dollars of How Now Brown Cow to make toddler dresses."

"Did you get her contact information? Does she want to teach a class?"

"I love how you think!"

"Same here Mak, same here."

Gloria and I were smiling like idiots. We had an entirely new revenue line to build into the business. I looked over my shoulder to make sure Ainsley wasn't looking. I flipped my middle fingers up and did an awkward little dance. "Screw you, Travis."

"What was that?"

I clasped my hands together and angelically turned to Gloria. "My mother sent my asshole brother out here to look at our books. She doesn't think this is a realistic business to open."

Gloria put her hands on her hips. "Jennifer Underwood is getting a phone call from me. Does she think that I have so much money I can just throw it away?"

I sighed. "In her mind, it's a hobby store. She said as much when she was out helping us set up. Meaning the store is your hobby and not a legitimate business. I told Travis to stuff it. He doesn't get to analyze a business that's been open for a few weeks, especially one in an industry he doesn't fathom. Mom never did crafts, of any kind. I don't think either of them realizes it's a multibillion-dollar industry."

"Well, it's a good thing that I do, and that you have such a good creative eye. Tapping into the stay-at-home mom market might be what we need to be able to advance our online presence timeline up."

My phone began ringing. Pulling it from my pocket, I looked at the caller ID. It was Holden. "I should take this."

I stepped back into the classroom area. "Are you calling to tell me you're coming home?"

There was a low groan on the other end of the call.

"Holden?"

"Sorry, I have to go in for surgery."

"What? Holden, what's going on?"

There was silence and then another voice. "Hi, is this Makenzie? I'm a nurse here at New Haven General. Holden asked if I could let you know what was going on. He's on some pain meds right now. So, talking isn't as comprehensive as he thinks it is."

"Okay, what's going on?" I asked slowly. My stomach cramped and I could only imagine the worst things possible.

"Something has gone awry with one of the plates in his leg. They'll be operating on him tonight to fix everything and remove it."

"By 'fix everything and remove it,' you aren't talking about amputating his leg, are you?"

"No," she laughed. "They're going to remove the plate. Oh, here he wants to talk to you."

There was a rustle and then heavy breathing.

"Holden?"

"I'm sorry. I owe you dinner." He didn't quite get full words out. Talking to him was very much like talking to Ainsley when she was first learning her words.

"Call me when you get out of surgery and remember to, okay?"

He muttered something that sent lightning through my body. It sounded a lot like I love you, but it was so garbled it could have been anything. The call ended and I stared at my phone for a while.

"I love you too."

26

HOLDEN

3 weeks later...

I grit my teeth together as I stood on both feet. It was less of a pain but more of a discomfort. A familiar discomfort that I had thought I would never have to experience again. I didn't have a cane to help me move, I had crutches.

"You only need to walk down the hall and back," my physiotherapist said.

"That's what you said last time."

"Well, it is a convenient length. Your mother's house is well suited for your recovery."

"I swear you have conspired to make this hall longer this morning," I called out as I limped my way down.

"You are getting steadier. How's the pain been?"

"An almost constant dull ache. Am I crazy or do I feel it more this time?" I slowly turned at the end of the hall and began my crutch walk back.

"Last time your arm was also fresh out of surgery."

"And my ribs, and a concussion, I would think that would put me in more pain."

"You probably were in more pain. I bet you were also on more pain management medication."

I took a tentative step. I winced.

"Next time pop a few acetaminophens before you go for a walk. That will help take the edge off. I think you are good until next week."

I shook my head.

"Not good?" he asked.

"I'm going back to Nantucket. I've been gone entirely too long." I had been stuck at my mother's house recovering from emergency surgery to replace one of the plates in my leg. In what the doctor described as a freak one in a million chance, the plate cracked, and an infection tried to move in. After he got me cleaned up, with new hardware, he suggested with my luck that I should consider buying a lottery ticket next.

Being in New Haven gave the lawyers more than enough time to discover more questionable business practices my father had engaged in. It was suddenly my job to clean up his mess. It really cut deep to know that he had tried to defraud the very government that I had served. Fortunately, we had more than enough money, and a deal was brokered to pay the back taxes while a forensic accountant came in and attempted to locate the funds that had to be hidden somewhere.

I felt guilty but I suggested they get in touch with my aunts. Maybe they knew something the rest of us didn't. I had to put my trust fund to work to make sure Mom's house was secure. Same with the property on Nantucket that I had transferred to my name. I wasn't going to let my mother suffer even more. It was bad enough that she lost my father, she didn't need to lose her way of life as well. Not when I had the means to keep her more than comfortable.

Penny had come through, and paperwork was ready and waiting for Ainsley's information to guarantee she would be taken care of. Makenzie may have never asked for child support, but I was prepared to provide it. I didn't even need a paternity test; I just needed some pertinent information such as birth date and social security number.

I needed to get some recovery behind me before I was stable enough to be on my own. I harbored fantasies of pulling IVs from my arms and walking out of the hospital against doctors' orders. There was something powerful thinking of oneself as a tough badass. If I had tried anything like that I would have simply ended up on my ass. I still barely had enough strength to grip the crutches with my left hand, and my leg could not support my weight, even a little bit.

I was stuck at my mom's while my body took its time mending. And I missed Makenzie the entire time, I even dreamed about her while under anaesthesia. We texted and even called, but three weeks of texting back and forth with Makenzie was barely enough to keep me satisfied. I longed to see her. I missed her in a way that I hadn't when I first joined up.

"Okay, Nantucket?" my therapist started, "I can find you a physiotherapist to work with there. I really think you need to keep working with someone. I know last time you were released on your own, but this has really set you back. Besides, I'm not convinced your arm is getting the work it needs."

"I'm fine," I brushed him off.

"Do this." He held his arm up and made a fist and then opened his hand flat with the palm face down.

That was easy and I was able to mimic his movements.

"Good, now do this." Not moving his arm, he rotated his wrist so that his palm was face up and his finger perfectly flat.

It was a strain, but I managed to get my thumb to point up, and my fingers all curled in toward my palm.

"Yeah, I'm giving you a referral." He pulled out a card and referenced his phone before writing down a phone number. "Seriously, if you want to regain full range of motion, you have got to work on that arm."

I took the number and promised to call. The next morning, I was limping off an airplane back on the island. I had my driver go straight to the quilt shop.

Ethan was out front with sawhorses, painting panels for something.

"How's it going? New signs?" I asked.

"Hi Holden, oh man, what happened to you?"

"They had to crack me back open and upgrade my hardware. What's all this?"

"Mak had a brilliant idea, and I'm finishing up the doors for a little play zone for Ainsley and other kids. It's really smart, and the shop has been full of moms with strollers for the past two weeks. It's like they have some kind of secret network and word got out they can shop and let the kids play. I've had one hell of a time getting space to do the work to put in the walls Mak asked for."

"Makenzie is a smart woman. That's a clever idea." I wanted to puff up my chest with how proud I was of her. I probably would have if I wasn't balancing my weight on one leg and a pair of crutches.

"Right? But I don't think her boyfriend agrees."

Cold water crashed through my veins. "Boyfriend?"

"Yeah, he's a big financier in New York. He's been here every weekend, and all they do is fight. The guy's a real asshole. Mom doesn't like him much either. Every time he shows up she makes me grab Ainsley and we leave."

"He's not here now, is he?"

"He's inside right now. They've been shouting at each other for like an hour. I know it's not my place but I've been telling people not to go inside."

"Where's Ainsley?"

He tilted his head indicating she was inside with Makenzie, and—I swallowed bile—her boyfriend. I looked in through the window. Makenzie was red-faced and animated with anger. I didn't recognize who she was yelling at, but he loomed over her and had hair only slightly darker than Ainsley's.

"Shit," I bit out. I was a fucking idiot.

"You want to know what I think?" Ethan asked.

"Sure, what do you think?" I knew what I thought, and it wasn't good.

"I think she ran away from him, but he found her. Mom told me Mak won't tell anyone who Ainsley's father is. I think it's this guy. He looks kind of like her. I mean Ainsley looks dead up like Mak, but she kind of looks like this guy too."

That's exactly what I was thinking. Fuck. I was an idiot. Makenzie had told me not to become invested in the idea that Ainsley was mine. And what did I go and do? I set up a fucking trust fund for some other guy's offspring.

I leaned on my crutches and seethed, glaring daggers into the back of the man who blocked me from Makenzie's view.

"You, okay?"

"What?" I turned to see Ethan looking at me with a puzzled expression on his face.

"I asked if you needed any help. You kind of froze up there."

I let out a heavy breath. "Just planning my next move."

"I thought you and Mak had something going, but this guy…"

"Mak and I are just old friends, nothing more. I'll be seeing you around."

I turned and hobbled back to the car. "Stop at the package store, would you?" I needed booze and lots of it. I had an ache in my chest that no pain killer was going to be able to touch.

27

MAKENZIE

There was a certain thrill that came with every fabric delivery. Anticipation built in my belly. The box knife slicing through the tape and opening was better than Christmas morning– least it was since becoming an adult. The brown cardboard gave way, opening to reveal a splash of color.

I was extra excited because this box contained the new line from Kate Bassett. Her sense of color was so different from other designers. She was young and cutting edge. Her personality really showed through in the designs full of hidden surprises and unexpected color combinations.

I made ridiculously appreciative noises as I pulled the bolts of fabric from the box and tore the plastic coverings from them.

"Mak, you sound like you're having really good sex."

My eyes went wide, and I felt the blush bloom on my cheeks.

"Gloria!" I chastised. "There are customers in the store."

"And everyone is looking at you. But trust me, we all understand. This new line is more satisfying than sex."

"I don't know about that," I giggled and blushed more as I thought about Holden's mouth on me. The fabric was pretty, but it did not reduce me to nothing but quivering good the way he did.

"We should double our order. I can already tell this is going to be a popular line."

"Do you think we will really sell that much?" It wasn't as if Kate Bassett was flying off our shelves. I held up a bolt with fairies and strawberries in the design. "This one will make the most adorable dress for Ainsley."

Gloria raised her brows and gave me a knowing look.

"Oh, I get it." She was right. If I was already looking at fabric for dresses for my little girl, so would other moms. We were going to need more stock, and the limited-edition lines always sold out fast. "I should make up a sample, shouldn't I?"

"Make two, one for her to wear, and one to put on the wall. I'll put in a second order for more fabric tomorrow when I go over inventory."

Gloria laughed at me. "Speaking of sex, how is your young man?"

"Gloria!" I was mortified, until I realized she was teasing me, and not digging for gossip to share with Mom. "Last I heard from him he was coming home. And then radio silence. I was really worried that something went wrong, but there were no small craft accidents reported. He's not responding to any of my texts or returning my calls. I'm not blocked because I can leave messages. I just don't understand. Maybe he's hurt worse that he is willing to admit."

The bell over the door jingled and we both looked up, ready to greet whoever walked in the door. Ethan struggled with the stroller, trying to get it through the door.

Gloria stepped over to hold the door for him. "Have you gone by his house? Is he even on the island?"

"Is who on the island?" Ethan asked.

"Holden. He's not responding to any of my messages."

"Yeah, he's back. I just saw him the other day. You were arguing with that guy, so he didn't want to come in. Actually, you know that whole arguing in the store scared off a lot of customers."

I closed my eyes as my world folded in around me. I was so fucking sick of my brother. I breathed hard through my nose and squashed down every single cuss word I wanted to yell. I wasn't a violent person, but Travis had me wanting to bash him.

The bells chimed again, I struggled to have a pleasant look on my face. I felt like hitting my brother for so many things, I couldn't even form a list. Keeping the glare out of my eyes was beyond me. Instead of staring death beams from my eyes, I forced my focus back down to the fabric. Gloria could be the happy shop greeter.

"Oh, you."

My head shot up, and I looked at who Gloria had greeted in such a dismissive fashion.

Travis.

I pinched my mouth shut and narrowed my eyes.

"We should go," Gloria said.

"No, you stay. We are the ones that need to leave. I'm embarrassed to learn that our argument the other day frightened customers away." I turned to Travis and pointed out the door.

I pinched the bridge of my nose as I followed him out. He stopped and leaned on the front of a car, parked directly in front of the shop.

"Is that even your car?"

He folded his arms and glanced down at the car. "Rental," he said with a shrug.

"Why are you even here? Don't you have a job in New York?"

165

"Mom said you're mad at her, so I came out to see what was up."

I could feel the anger building. My blood pressure was spiking, and I shook with blinding rage.

"You asshole. You know exactly why I'm upset with her. You could have told her yourself; you didn't need to come all the way out here."

He was so calm it was infuriating. He pulled out his phone and hit a few buttons and then held it out so I could hear the call.

"Hi Mom, I'm with Mak."

I glared at him with all my impotent rage. He had called Mom.

"Makenzie? Honey, why are you so mad at me?"

"Really? We're doing this? Mom, you're on speaker phone in the middle of the sidewalk. I don't know what game Travis is playing right now—"

"Now, Makenzie," Mom cut me off. "Your brother is just trying to be helpful."

I glared at him, he responded with a smirk. I wanted to smack that expression from his face. I kept my eyes on Travis, even though I spoke to the phone.

"Mom," I started. I hated being manipulated this way. I took a deep breath. "I'm angry because you sent Travis to check on my business without any regards to the fact that I have a business partner, and Travis is not knowledgeable about the sewing crafts industry."

"But he's so good with money, and he offered."

I was speechless. A long moment of silence passed.

"Makenzie?" Mom asked.

Travis's smirk grew bigger, and then he began laughing. "You are too fucking easy to manipulate."

I swallowed hard. "Mom, I'm not mad at you, but I might just kill my brother."

I hit his phone ending the call.

"You complete asshole. All of this was for some "gotcha!" prank? You have been a completely annoying prick for weeks. You scared off customers the last time you were here. My home is not your private vacation rental. You really aren't happy unless you are making me miserable, are you? You almost ruined my relationship with our mother, and you think it's funny? You've probably ruined my relationship with Holden—"

Travis surged to his feet. "What about Holden? You haven't been seeing him, have you? I warned him to stay away from you."

It was my turn to cross my arms and look smug. "It's a small island, Travis. Of course, we see each other."

Travis spun without a word and yanked open the car door.

"Where the hell do you think you're going?"

"I'm going to kill that son of a bitch."

Travis backed the rental car into traffic without even looking. Tires squealed as he took off. I stared after him for a moment longer than I should have. Realization of Travis's anger at Holden finally shook me to action. I sprinted into the shop and scrambled under the counter.

"Where's my purse?"

"What's going on?"

"I have to stop Travis. I think he's really going to hurt Holden." I ran back out the door, keys in hand.

My car was down the block, it was going to take forever to get to it, and then out to Holden's house. I ran through stop signs and drove entirely too fast. I tried to call Holden, but he wasn't answering me. I roared with all my pent-up rage at my brother.

I would hate him forever and a day if he hurt Holden. Maybe if Holden wasn't recovering from a second surgery after his accident, it would be a fair fight. Or not, in Holden's favor. Both men were tall, and worked out, but Holden hadn't fully recovered yet.

My mini van skidded to a stop in the gravel at the end of Holden's driveway.

Travis and Holden were facing off. Holden pointed a crutch at Travis, keeping him back.

I jumped from my car.

Travis was yelling. "…. all those women you slept with in college."

"That's bullshit. The real issue here is I get back from being stuck on the mainland because of some surgery, only to find out that my kid might not be mine, and it's going to take a court order to get a paternity test... Who is your sister's boyfriend? Is he the kid's father? Maybe you need to rethink who you call a player. It's not me."

Just then Holden's eyes locked with mine. The pain I saw there was a mirror to my own. I couldn't do this anymore. I turned and climbed back in the van. I couldn't get away from Holden, or my brother fast enough.

28

HOLDEN

Plans for leaving the island got jumbled in my head with emotions. Makenzie had been so hot and eager in my arms only weeks ago, how could she have forgotten to tell me about a boyfriend? Had the chemistry between us clouded her better judgement? At any time in the past few weeks, she could have mentioned the guy in any of the text messages she sent.

I should have turned right around and gotten on a plane back to Connecticut. But a nagging gut instinct kept me on the island. Maybe I wanted to run into her and not-so-passively but aggressively mention that I saw that man she was with and confront her about him being her daughter's father.

I was a fucking chump, is what I was. I had convinced myself that Ainsley was mine. I had created an entire fantasy world where we ended up together, a happy little family. All the activities I would do to burn through this frustration had been taken from me. No weight training, and sure as hell no running. Instead, I punished myself by limping up and down the fucking drive until I was too exhausted to think at all. I ended my days by washing down a pain pill with whiskey. I saw no reason to fake being concerned about mixing substances or avoiding dependency-like behaviors.

Fuck it all.

I was a human ball of hate as I crutch limped up my drive and then returned toward the house. I stopped when an unfamiliar green sedan pulled in.

"What the fuck do you think you're doing?"

I turned to see Travis Underwood storming toward me.

"Physical therapy asshole. Go away."

"I'm not going anywhere until you understand that I don't want you anywhere near my sister, or anyone in my family. Ever."

"Fuck off, Travis." I was too tired to stand around arguing with him. I started to place the crutches so that I could turn around and finish limping my way back to my booze and pills and oblivion for the rest of the day.

"When did you go from having any woman you wanted, to my sister? Even after I told you to keep your distance."

He took an aggressive step forward. I lifted my crutch to fend him off. "You're not my mother or my commanding officer, you don't get to tell me what to do. Maybe you should have told your sister to stay away from me."

"Trust me, I did. You don't seem to understand the issue here, Holden."

It was too late by the time I saw Makenzie. The words were out of my mouth accusing her of being indiscriminate and sleeping around. I didn't believe them as soon as I said them. It didn't matter who the child's biological father was. I was in love with Makenzie. I wanted to be the father to all of her children.

The look of pain she gave me was enough to bring me to my knees begging for forgiveness. She was in her van and speeding down the street before I could take back my words.

"Makenzie!"

I took one pitiful crutch-assisted limp forward.

With every fiber of my being, I hated that I couldn't run after her. I rounded on Travis to the best of my ability. I hated these fucking crutches, I hated my fucking leg, and I hated that incompetent airman who lost control of his plane. I really hated the man standing in front of me.

"You can't be seriously trying to run after her?"

"Get out of my way." If limping was all I could do, then damn it, I was going to limp my way to her house. She deserved an explanation more than I needed to know who Ainsley's father was.

Logically, what I should have done was pick up my phone and call the car service. Hell, what I should have done was finally call her back. But logic wasn't my friend at the moment, and I wasn't thinking clearly.

Travis shook his head. "I told you to stay away from her."

"That's not something I can do."

"Oh, God, don't come up with some lame excuse and tell me that you love her. That's ridiculous. We're talking about Mak."

"I know we are talking about Makenzie, and I do love her. I have for a very long time. You wouldn't understand."

He thrust his arm out and pointed in the direction of their house. "You're right, I don't understand. Of all the people you could be with I will never understand. Man, you always had your choice of women."

I shook my head. He was wrong. "There has only ever been one woman for me. I don't know why you think I was some kind of playboy. Have you ever seen me with anyone? No. You were the one sleeping your way through the student body. Not me."

I took a limping step away.

"You ruined our friendship."

Leaning heavily on my crutches, I turned back around.

"How? Explain it to me. As far as I know, we were friends right up to the point where I announced I joined the Army. And then you went south on me. You ruined our friendship."

"You were dating my sister! Mak is, has, and will always be trash. I don't know why I'm the only one who can see that."

"Don't ever call her trash." If I wasn't so fucking weak, I would have planted my fist in his face.

"I can't believe you are standing there defending her to me now when you were just whining about needing a paternity test, so she didn't saddle you with paying for some other guy's brat."

He ran his hands through his hair and walked in a tight circle.

"She's playing you, Holden. She has been the entire time. You were my best friend, you could have had anyone else, and I wouldn't have said a thing."

"What the hell is your problem with her, Travis?"

"You have got to be kidding me. You were there. Every fucking birthday party had to have a princess. She was always trying to insert herself into everything I ever did."

"She's your sister, she wanted you to like her. You're seriously still mad that you share the same birth date? As if she had control over that. Grow the fuck up."

"No, you grow the fuck up. She ruined my life."

"How?"

"She was born."

I let out a heavy breath and shook my head. "Jesus Travis, do you ever listen to yourself? Seek therapy. Seriously. You have issues, and I'm done letting them get in my way. So, what if I was dating Makenzie? We were together for years before you found out. It never affected our friendship."

"You were sneaking around and didn't tell me?"

"Because we knew you would act like a little bitch if you found out."

"She's not fucking good enough for you. She wasn't some innocent little girl you left behind when you went off to play Army man."

A growl started low in my throat.

"You weren't even gone more than six or seven months before she went and had some other guy's baby."

"What did you just say?" I tried to wrap my head around the numbers he said.

"That kid of hers was born the February after you left. She didn't waste any time hooking up with some guy who knocked her up."

I spoke slowly because I needed to maintain some level of control. I felt like I was going to burst out of my skin.

"I left in August. And you're saying the kid was born in February, and you think it's some other guy's child?"

"Not unless you were fucking Mak, and I know that wasn't happening."

I blew air out in a long low whistle.

"What's your fucking problem this time?"

I laughed. "You're an idiot. How long does it take to make a baby? Do you even know? Because unless Ainsley was born prematurely, she is definitely mine. Look, I don't know what you said or did to Makenzie to keep her away from me but fuck you. I've lost years with her, and my daughter."

"How do you even know that kid is yours? Weren't you just demanding a paternity test? Make up your fucking mind."

"Really Travis? Did you skip basic biology in school? Babies take nine fucking months. And if Ainsley's birthday is in February, she was conceived in..." I closed my eyes and ran a fast calculation. "Sometime in June. Trust me, that means she's mine. I could maybe understand you being pissed off because I knocked your sister up and ran away, but this other shit you're talking about is one for the books, it's so ludicrous it's almost funny."

Travis visually deflated in front of me.

"Mak refused to tell anyone who the father is. I guess I never really thought about it. I got it in my head that she wasn't good enough for you. Having someone else's baby proved my point. Fuck!" He punched the air and stomped around.

I was too tired to keep arguing with him.

"Your sister has always been the only one for me. And you were better than a best friend. You were my brother from another mother. You've hurt too many people with your pettiness. Get off my property."

29

MAKENZIE

I stopped long enough to pick up Ainsley from the shop and tell Gloria I needed to leave for a few days. We were on the very next ferry off the island. I drove on autopilot, not sure where I was going at first, I just needed to get away from the island and the men on it.

I felt like a fool having fallen for Holden a second time. I didn't know where else I could go, or what I was really doing. I needed someplace to hide and lick my wounds while I figured everything out. I pulled up to my childhood home in upstate New York by dinner time.

Mom was out the door and by the van before I had even had a chance to call and let her know we would be there. Without a word, she wrapped her arms around me and let me cry. I didn't indulge myself for long, because I didn't want to worry Ainsley.

"How's my best girl?" Mom asked as she opened the side door and began unbuckling her granddaughter.

I wiped my eyes, put on a fake smile, and followed them inside. I didn't talk about why I was at home suddenly, without warning, without luggage. Mom showed great restraint and didn't ask me any questions until after we got Ainsley put to bed for the night.

"Okay, honey, you want to tell me what's going on? You didn't drive all this way because of a little teasing from your brother?"

I sat in the kitchen while Mom washed dishes. She never let anyone else clean her kitchen. No one ever did it to her standards, so we learned to stay out of her way.

"If you defend Travis, I'll wake Ainsley up and go to a hotel." I didn't hide the bitterness in my voice.

"You know he does those things to get a rise out of you."

"No Mom, he doesn't. Maybe when he was a kid, but he still does it. My emotions are not for his entertainment. Maybe coming here was a bad idea. You never defended me against him."

"What for? Your brother was showing a little sibling rivalry."

"He tried to get me so angry with you that I stopped talking to you, and you want to brush that off as sibling rivalry?" I folded my arms on the table and did my best to bury my head. I came home for support, instead, I was having to fight Travis all over again, and he wasn't even here.

"I think you need to leave it, Jennifer," Dad said.

I felt his big warm hand on the back of my neck. He squeezed, providing some much-needed non-verbal support.

"Travis has always been hard on her. Maybe too hard."

"You know how boys are."

"I do, I was one once. I also know how men are, and Travis is acting like a child."

"Fine, I'll drop it. Mak, as long as you're home, I need you to help me clean out a few things tomorrow."

I lifted my head and wearily looked at her. That was Mom, conscripting me to do work the second I was home. I nodded and put my head back down.

"Go to bed, kiddo," Dad said. "You've had a hard day."

He could tell, and I really hadn't said much more than I was sick of Travis. They didn't even know my situation with Holden and how that felt like an anchor tied to my feet dragging me down, while Travis kept stepping on my fingers, not letting me pull myself up.

The next morning, I woke up feeling woozy. I stumbled my way down to the kitchen, following the alluring aroma of fresh coffee. Mom already had Ainsley dressed and eating breakfast.

I kissed my daughter on top of her head and poured myself some of the delicious coffee.

"I need your help going through some boxes we pulled out of Travis's old room."

"Mom," I whined.

"No, it's perfect for you. "You don't have an emotional attachment to his belongings. You'll have detached objectivity when it comes to what we should keep and box up for him, or what to toss."

"It's Travis's crap, make him do it."

"It's not much stuff. You can do it while you're here. You didn't mention last night how long you were staying."

"I don't know yet. Only a few days. I can't leave Gloria with the store all by herself, that wouldn't be fair."

I took a long sniff of the coffee, it smelled… suddenly I was gagging. The coffee was rank. I pinched my lips together and ran for the down-stairs bathroom. I wretched, even though there wasn't anything in my stomach to come back up.

While rinsing my face, I tried to remember the last time I had felt sick like this. I let out a small manic laugh. Almost four years ago exactly. It had been summer then too. I hurried to the kitchen and told Mom I needed to run to the drug store.

She nodded with understanding. "That time of the month?"

"Yeah," I laughed nervously.

As I threw on the clothes, I had worn the day before. I tried to remember the last 'time of the month' I had. I sat on my bed in shock. It had been before that night on the yacht, and that was over a month ago.

I scrambled for my keys and raced out the door to buy a pregnancy test. I couldn't believe this. The first time I had been with a man in four years, and I got pregnant again. But we had used a condom. Condoms failed occasionally; Ainsley was proof of that.

Holden wasn't going to believe this. Hell, I had him convinced that Ainsley wasn't his, even though he had figured it out. Now I was going to have to prove to him that this one was his too. What kind of a mess had I gotten myself into?

I swept through the drug store and bought the test I needed. I used their restroom to take the test, too impatient to drive home. I danced anxiously as I waited for the lines to appear confirming what my body was telling me.

Congratulations Makenzie, you let Holden knock you up again. It wasn't as if I could keep the father a secret a second time. Not that I had ever wanted to do that the first time. It just sort of happened.

I drove home in a haze of confusion.

"All better? Here, can you sort through this mess?" Mom wasted no time and as soon as I got home, she had me going through my brother's belongings.

I didn't know what to do with half of the things, while the rest of the stuff was obviously for the trash bin. I folded all of his old concert shirts, thinking he would want those, while other random articles of clothing I put in a pile for donating. While I worked my thoughts bounced back and forth between extremes.

I couldn't help but feel like Mom was setting me up for Travis to hate me even more. She wouldn't have to deflect the blame for cleaning from herself onto me, Travis would do so naturally. I wanted to be done with him, and never have to speak with him again. I also knew that wasn't a reality with this family.

The other extreme my thoughts got lost in was Holden and that look of hurt anger on his face. I couldn't help but wallow in self-pity. He had hated me at that moment, believed that I had slept with someone else after he left for the Army. I could have avoided everything if I had simply admitted that Ainsley was his the second, he confronted me with it. I couldn't redo the past. How did I fix the future?

I opened a shoebox full of old letters. I hesitated for a second before tossing the whole thing into the keep pile. I never figured Travis for a romantic, keeping old letters. Curiosity got the best of me, and I pulled one of the letters out.

I had to reread the address several times. It was addressed to me. I flipped the envelope over to see if I recognized the return address written on the back. It was a weird APO Box number. No, this couldn't be. I looked at the cancellation date on the stamp. It had been mailed almost four years ago.

I riffled through the rest of the box. Almost all of the letters were to me, here at the house. I had never seen any of these. My blood ran cold when I picked up the next envelope. That was my handwriting, and it was addressed to Holden.

"What the fuck?"

I flipped one of the envelopes addressed to me over. The address I used for Holden looked remarkably similar. But not quite.

The one Travis had given to me, saying Holden wanted me to write to him, was "Wells APO" with a New York, NY destination. I hadn't thought anything of it at the time. Travis had told me Army addresses were different, that APO meant Army Post Office. In my grief, I had trusted him.

I tore into one of the letters addressed to me and began reading. I covered my mouth and sobbed. Holden had written to me, had loved me, had been as hurt as I was that I wasn't returning his letters.

30

HOLDEN

The cotton button down and jacket combined with the climate control in the building was making my skin itch. I didn't know how anyone worked in those conditions. I needed air, lots of it. I didn't care if it was laced with gas fumes or fresh— fresh was better— but anything was better than that sterile personality-free environment.

It smacked of the same homogeneous neutrality the lawyer's offices had where I had spent my morning. I had refused to wear a tie for the lawyers. I couldn't imagine voluntarily wearing one on a daily basis. Every man I saw walking in and out of the building had worn one. I shrugged my shoulders trying to get comfortable on the elevator ride up. The height didn't bother me, everything else did.

I gave my name to the receptionist and then stood, waiting. Mentally I paced back and forth, while actually I stayed in one spot leaning on my crutches. I didn't bother sitting because I didn't want anyone to watch the struggle of getting back to my feet.

Travis came around the corner, moving like he was on wheels. His suit jacket buttoned; a red power tie knotted at his throat. I suppressed a shudder. This was no kind of working situation for me, but he seemed to revel in it.

"Holden, I was surprised when they announced you were here. Let's have a seat." He had a wide smile on his face and was all charm and personality. He gestured at the lobby couch.

I shook my head. "Some place with a little more privacy, I think."

"Sure, sure. I didn't want you to have to walk too far. You made it all the way up here, I thought you might be tired."

He oozed insincerity. I didn't trust him, but I needed his help. I was exhausted, my leg ached and my arm throbbed from having to support my weight on the crutches. I wasn't going to let him know any of that. He already had me at a disadvantage.

He leaned over the receptionist desk and said something. She smiled and with a coy tilt of her head and fanning of her eye lashes, she looked something up on the computer in front of her. Travis had to have been pleased with what she told him. He hit her desk with a double tap and turned to me holding an arm out.

"We can use one of the small conference rooms right over here. My office is on the far side of the floor. No need to make you walk more than we have to."

He waited until I was inside the conference room to speak. I bounced on one foot, pulling a second chair to me while trying to balance the crutches against the table. It was a dance I wasn't well versed in, and the crutches slid in my way more than once.

"What are you doing here, Holden?" He stood by the door with his arms folded over his chest. That was the Travis I knew and hated.

"You said you wanted to fix things. I haven't heard from you in days."

"You could have called," he scoffed.

"Yeah, I could have. I was already in the city so I decided to swing by and see what you knew."

"What has you brought you to New York, if not to see me?" He unbuttoned his jacket and finally sat down.

I tapped the table and thought about how much I did want to tell him. How much could I trust him after all these years of building resentment? I took a long look at him; he had been my best friend for years.

"You really want to regain my friendship?"

He nodded.

"I haven't been able to run after Makenzie because there is a situation with my father's estate I'm juggling. All I know is she is out of town, and she hasn't come back yet. I need your help in locating her."

He nodded. "That's easy enough. She's at home with our parents."

"You know this for certain?"

"I spoke with my mother last night. She wants me to stop picking on my sister," he scoffed.

"Travis, I wouldn't exactly call what you do picking on her."

I fumbled with the crutches and cussed when I dropped one of them for a second time. I was back on my feet without some struggle. I took a step to leave.

"Where are you off to now?"

I paused before I reached the conference room door. "I'm headed to your parents' to get Makenzie."

Travis stood and buttoned his jacket like a reflex. "Let me drive. I messed up, I owe you both and should help to fix this. You can tell me about the problem with your dad's estate on the drive."

I expected Travis to drive something low, sleek, and bright red. I was surprised when we walked up to a luxury vehicle in the parking garage. He adjusted the seat in the back and held the crutches so I could get in and sit behind him. For a moment it was like having my old friend back.

We didn't talk for the first part of the trip as he navigated out of the city. Once we were on the freeway and traffic thinned, he opened up the engine and let his car go. I understood why he drove this car, the speed, the smoothness of the ride, the quiet power of the engine. It was understated and in control. Pretty much how I thought Travis wanted to be seen as.

"Why were you in New York, Holden? What's going on with the estate?"

I laid everything out. I saw no reason to hold back. The investigation contractors had a hot lead we needed to follow up with in person. It involved a safety deposit box.

"There was this big production, we had to exchange passwords. Mom found a key in Dad's things. It smacked of intrigue and felt so unreal, like it was some kind of movie."

"So, what happened?"

"Not a damned thing. It was a dead end. The box held a few savings bonds, and a copy of my dad's birth certificate. We're talking about five hundred."

"Five hundred what? Grand? Million?"

I laughed. "No, five hundred. Five zero zero. He paid more in rent on the thing over the years than what he was keeping secure inside it. It's back to the beginning on the investigation."

"So, you're saying your dad had to have some investments or secret accounts where he was syphoning funds off to? Have you considered that he spent the money?"

"Of course, but the amount of money we are talking about, and his spending habits don't match up. Hell, Mom's spending habits don't support what we're talking about."

"Your dad didn't have a girlfriend, did he?"

"Travis, you knew my dad, did he seem like the type to have a side chick?"

"I think we never truly know people, especially when they want to keep something a secret. I had no clue about you and Mak until she said something. And we lived together. How the hell would I know if your dad had an entire second family he was hiding?"

He had a point.

"I'm pretty good at sniffing out money. I could help"

I did not doubt that for a minute. It's not like he could do any more damage than what Dad had done. We— the company, me, and Mom— were already paying back taxes. Discovering the location and having access to the missing money wasn't going to hurt any worse than we already were.

"I'll put you in contact with the team at Clay and Silverstein. Let them know I'm bringing you in. I should also put you in contact with Penny. She's on the legal team at the company."

"Penny? Sounds like an old lady."

"Penny, as in don't even think about seducing her, I like her and want to keep her in my employment. I'd have to hate you all over again if you fucked that up."

"It sounds like you haven't stepped up into running things at your old man's company."

"I haven't. It's too soon."

"Too soon, or you aren't ready?"

"I can barely walk, I sure as hell am in no shape to be in an office. Too soon, not ready, or don't fucking want to, it's all the same."

The conversation drifted back to silence once Travis reached our destination.

"How do you want to do this? I can go straight to the house, or…"

"I think neutral territory would be best. Let's find a restaurant or a hotel where you can drop me, and then see if you can get her to agree to come talk."

MAKENZIE

"Mak! Makenzie, someone is here to see you." Mom hovered just outside my bedroom.

"What? Who? No one knows I'm here." I folded a few items of clothing from the morning's laundry. It was a good thing I hadn't moved my entire wardrobe when I went to live on Nantucket. I had something to wear once I got home. It was a different issue for Ainsley. The clothes that had been left behind for her no longer fit. I hadn't realized just how much she had grown until we tried to get her dressed on our second day here.

Mom was perfectly happy to buy her new dresses. I was perfectly happy not to have to buy anything new for myself. I needed to put the clean laundry away, and seriously think about returning to my home and my business on Nantucket. It was time to grow up again. If there was nothing left between Holden and me, so be it. It would hurt. A lot. I still cried from my initial loss of him four years ago. I cried more from whatever had just gone wrong between us recently.

I put the laundry down and followed her down the hall and through the rest of the house to the living room. I wasn't paying attention at first. I had no idea who could be waiting for me. For a split second, I thought Holden had found me. My nerves danced at the idea.

That lasted until I saw who was sitting in the living room. He sat very formally as if he too hadn't grown up and tortured me in this very house. He sat like a nervous guest and not the favorite son. Travis stood and fastened his jacket. He was grossly proper.

I spun on my heel, only Mom had gotten behind me and put her hands up stopping me.

"I'm not talking to him."

"You don't have to talk, but you should listen."

"No, why should I? He ruined my life."

"You're being dramatic, Makenzie."

"No, she's not," Travis interrupted.

I spun back to stare at him. Had I heard him correctly? "Come again?"

"What are you talking about Travis? What is all of this?" Mom crossed her arms and stared at him almost with the same intensity that I was.

He let out a heavy breath. "Makenzie is right. I purposefully got in the way of a relationship. I fucked things up."

I wanted a recording of him admitting I was right. I wanted to play it over and over again. It was a victory, only I wasn't exactly sure how I had won it.

"Travis, there's no need for that kind of language."

"Yes, there is," I said. "He's grossly underestimating the damage he's done. He ruined everything and then spent the last four years doing everything he could to make it worse. I found the letters, Travis. You kept him from me. Why? What did I ever do that was so bad that you intentionally kept us apart?"

"Who are we talking about? Who did Travis keep you away from, honey?"

I looked at Mom. I knew that Holden and I had been sneaking around, but I honestly thought most people would have figured it out.

"He kept Holden away from me."

"But Holden joined the Army. Travis, what is she talking about? You didn't have anything to do with that did you?"

Travis shook his head. "I didn't, but I did interfere once he joined. I thought I was losing a good friend, so I lashed out and, in the end, I did ruin that friendship. And I blamed Makenzie entirely for it when she hadn't done a thing."

I slowly clapped. "You finally clued in. But how does that help me in any way?"

He held his hand out to me. I sneered at it. I don't know what he thought was going to happen. Did he think he could walk in here and say, 'I'm sorry' and he'd suddenly be my favorite older brother? That I would magically forgive him for ruining the past four years of my life and harassing me for the past few weeks about my business?

That was not what was going to happen. I had a good twenty-five plus years of resentment built up that needed to be sifted through. It wasn't going to disappear in a puff of happy sparkly glitter.

"I need to show you something," he said.

I crossed my arms and shook my head. I didn't trust him.

"I messed up Mak. I have a lot to atone for. Please…"

"Why now? What's different today from last week when you were harassing me over my books? Why should I trust you?"

"Go with him, Makenzie," Mom urged.

I spun to face her. "If you knew half of what I've put up with from him, you wouldn't be telling me to go with him but to run in the opposite direction. He hid the letters Holden wrote to me and gave me a fake address so that he could keep me from writing to Holden."

"Holden again," she sighed. "Why does it matter? Why would you and Holden exchange letters when he joined the Army? He was Travis's friend."

"Mom," I practically yelled. I wanted to shake her. Instead, I pinched the bridge of my nose. "Holden is Ainsley's father, that's why it matters. That's how he ruined my life." I pointed at Travis like this was some courtroom drama and I was identifying the culprit.

Mom put her hand to her mouth to cover a gasp. She dropped into the nearest chair. Her gaze bounced back and forth between me and Travis.

"Oh Travis, what have you done?"

My brother at least had the decency to look guilty.

"If I go with you..."

"It will be worth your time. I promise."

I set my mouth in a firm line and nodded in agreement. "I'll go." I turned to Mom. "Ainsley is asleep right now. She'll want a snack when she gets up."

"I know, juice box, her bear, and two episodes of her show so she can wake up and not feel cranky. I do know how to take care of toddlers, Mak. Go with your brother, he came all this way for a reason."

I hesitated, but in the end, I grabbed my purse and followed Travis out to his car. We didn't speak and I didn't ask Travis any questions. I stared at my fingernails and was proud of myself that I hadn't attempted to rake them down my brother's smug face. Only he hadn't been smug at all. But I wasn't convinced that he was truly remorseful.

I kept my anger in reserve, waiting for this to be another one of his manipulative pranks.

"Holden and I had it out. He knew about Ainsley before I did, and I guess I was being pretty stupid." Travis said eventually.

"No, Travis. You were being mean." I turned to stare out the window. I didn't want to speak to him. I questioned why I had gotten in the car with him, to begin with.

The house was fairly far out in an upper-scale residential area. We grew up surrounded by homes with large properties and winding roads to get to any kind of shopping.

Travis drove like he knew these roads better than the back of his own hand. He cut through an industrial area that was a shortcut to get onto the main road that went past the local mall. He passed all of that and followed the road as it curved behind the cemetery.

"I don't need a tour of town. Where are we going?"

"Old Town."

Old Town was the tiny area that had once been the economic center of town. It was out of the way and tucked up against a small state park. The only things there were touristy-type shops. High-end and high-priced restaurants.

And the Grande, one of those hotels built at the turn of the last century. Built for luxury and opulence that had fallen into disrepair mid-century and would have been given over to ruins and ghost stories if the local conservationist hadn't run a long campaign to have it restored to its former glory, and better.

Travis eased his car up to the valet stand and got out. A valet opened my door.

I looked over the top of the car at Travis. "Why are we here?"

He nodded at the open doors, and I turned to look. I had to blink a few times to adjust my focus to the dim interior, but Holden was there propped up on crutches.

"I'll let Mom know you're okay and will be home tomorrow. I owe you this Mak, I've been a suck brother."

I couldn't have agreed more.

At some point between the car door closing and standing in front of Holden, I had started crying. He opened his arms to me, and I wrapped myself around him. I didn't want to let go ever again.

32

HOLDEN

The second I saw Travis's car pull up I struggled to my feet. If Makenzie didn't come to me of her own volition, I would go and get her. That didn't need to happen. As soon as she saw me, she started crying. She was in my arms soon enough. We didn't need words to know we were both sorry, and that we also forgave each other. We would share our words later, but right then, with her in my arms, we were good.

I gave Travis a nod and was aware that he got back in his car before I turned all of my attention to her. I let Makenzie cry, holding her, and stroking her hair. With my finger under her chin, I tipped her face up and claimed her lips. The kiss tasted of her salty tears.

"Hey, it's okay. I'm here now."

"Holden," she said my name in a breath. "I'm sorry."

"No, I'm sorry. I should have given you the chance to tell me, and not railroad you because I figured it out."

"You aren't mad?"

"I've got a room, let's talk there. More privacy." I didn't need the hotel staff gaping at us any more openly than they were. I'm sure the beautiful crying woman and the broken, crippled man in their lobby would give them more than enough to gossip over. Besides I wanted, no I needed to kiss Makenzie again, and that wasn't for prying eyes.

She nodded.

I gestured, indicating she should go ahead of me toward the elevator.

She shook her head. "I want to walk with you."

"I'm too slow. I—"

"No, Holden. I want to be by your side. On your own two feet or with crutches. Your speed is my speed. I'm not in a rush as long as we can be together."

I stopped and leaned on the crutches, drinking her in. In jeans that might have been a bit too tight on her full hips and a tee that had seen better days, with no makeup and her nose red from crying, she was more beautiful than I think she had ever been.

"Did I say something wrong?"

I shook my head. "You said everything right."

She wrapped her arms around my arm and leaned her head against me in the elevator, not putting any of her weight against me. I balanced on my good leg and shifted that crutch out of her way so I could wrap my arm around her shoulder and hold her close. She supported me for the awkward moment after the doors slid open and I needed both crutches again.

In the room I hobbled to the bed and sat down, leaning the crutches next to me. Makenzie picked them up and put them across the room.

"I might need those."

"Then I will get them for you. Holden"— she knelt down in front of me and held my hands— "You know that Ainsley is our daughter and that I never…"

We stared into each other's faces for a long moment.

"I love you. And I know you. I don't know how things went so wrong, but I want to fix them."

She looked over her shoulder at the door. She crossed the room and double-checked the locks before returning to sit next to me. With our fingers laced together, and her head on my shoulder she began talking.

"I didn't want Travis to be able to come in and ruin this. I know he's your friend, but he did his best to destroy everything between us."

"I know, he told me everything. And he hasn't been my friend for a long time, but we are going to see if that can get fixed."

"He told you about the letters?"

"What letters?"

She explained how she found all of the letters that we had written, describing the growing heartbreak as each one didn't get answered. How we both seemed to have hope that the next letter would get through, that we would be back together soon.

I pulled her into my lap and pressed my lips to her brow. "Did you tell me about Ainsley in those letters? Did you know before I left?"

She shook her head. "I found out the day you told me you were leaving. I couldn't ruin your dreams; you were so excited. No, I didn't tell you in the letters because telling you that you're going to be a father was something that I needed to do in person. Like this"— she cupped my cheek and looked deep into my eyes— "Holden, we're having a baby."

I chuckled. "I know, she's three, and she is the most beautiful little girl."

"Yeah, but I have another surprise for you, Holden."

"Is it" Don't tell me you are pregnant again?

"I am Holden, and this time I want you to be by my side for our first scan."

"Wow. I'll make sure of that, Makenzie. No one can take that away from me this time." Adrenaline surged through my body. Joy and love and too many emotions took my breath away. I kissed Makenzie hard.

We rolled into the middle of the bed. With my good arm, I propped myself above her. She looked up at me and ran her fingers through my hair.

"Why are you so happy?"

"Because I love you. Because you love me and are giving me children. Because we're together and nothing is going to get between us ever again."

She smiled and blushed. "There's something between us right now."

I lifted my brows in question.

"Too many clothes," she giggled.

She was right, and we made quick work of undressing each other. I wasn't wearing the compression sleeves over my injuries, since my clothes had hidden the scars from sight.

She didn't say anything, no gasps of horror when she saw the long angry red marks on my leg. Her gentle fingers over my skin were a soothing balm. It was as if her simple touch could ease the deep ache in my injured bones and remove my pain. I lay back and let her examine my scars, no longer worried about how she might see me as weak for having them.

She pressed me back and climbed up my body. Her breasts brushed against me in a sensual promise of pleasure. Her lips against mine were sweet perfection. Everything about her in my arms was better than a dream.

"I guess until you're back up to fighting weight, I get to drive this show." She straddled my hips and rubbed her heat against my cock.

"I think even after I fully recover, I might let you drive. The view from down here is so fucking hot." I reached up and captured her breasts in my hands.

With a satisfied sigh, she lowered onto me, accepting me into her body.

I let go of all thought and reveled in the sensation of this woman pressed against my body. Her full soft breasts in my hands, her hungry hips pressing and grinding against mine.

We were always good at this, our bodies knew exactly what the other person needed, desired. Her gasps and squeals as my touch drove her toward orgasm, lit me up. I was done for as soon as her inner walls began pulsing and sucking at me.

I dug my fingers into her thighs and pushed up, leveraging with my good leg. Makenzie threw back her head and braced against my chest. She cried out and spasmed around me. With a thrust of my hips, I overbalanced her, so she collapsed against me. I was too far gone in my own need. We hit the pinnacle of orgasm together.

She was limp against my chest, her body pressing me down. I wrapped my arms around her and held her to me. She was mine; I wasn't going to let her go ever again.

"Marry me?"

"What? Like this, now?" She laughed and wiggled against me.

"Now would be good. But I always thought you would want a big wedding. You know, show off to the world that you snagged me."

"Oh, you think you're some kind of a catch, do you?"

I shook my head. "No, but you are. And I would be so proud to give you a big show-off wedding if that's what you want. I'd be happy getting married at the courthouse tomorrow as long as you are mine."

She rolled to the side and lifted up to look at me. "I've always been yours, only yours."

My chest tightened with emotion. I hooked my hand around the back of her neck and dragged her back down to kiss me. I vowed at that moment, that I would only be hers for the rest of our lives.

33

EPILOGUE

MAKENZIE

One year later...

I blinked tears out of my vision. I couldn't help it, I kept crying. Every time I thought about what we were doing. With every realization that Holden was finally going to be my husband, I started leaking again. I looked up and pressed a finger below my eye trying to get the tears to stop. I hadn't thought I would be a teary bride, but I was a total crying mess.

I didn't want Holden's first view of me as his bride to be one where my makeup was streaking down my face.

"Are you ready, kiddo?" Dad asked. I gave him a nod, too nervous to speak.

"Is it time?" Ainsley danced in a circle, spinning in her flower girl dress.

"It's time. Remember just like we practised. Don't run," I admonished as she hurried down the aisle. She stopped and looked back at me, and then ran back, only to turn around and walk slowly with her step-together-step pace as we had practised so many times. She took do-overs seriously, and she walked down that aisle as if she hadn't gotten excited and started off running.

A light chuckle spread through our guests.

I was already halfway down the aisle when Travis tapped Holden to turn around. They stood at the front of the chapel, waiting for me to arrive. All of the emotions he felt were clear and bold on his face, from smiling with laughter as Ainsley started to dance to how much he loved me when we finally made eye contact.

A burbling coo drew my attention to Mom as I approached the front of the small chapel. She held Meadow, who at only a few months old was smiling as if she knew what was going on. She probably simply liked all the music and sparkling lights. I was happy that my baby girl wasn't upset and could be here.

Dad literally handed me over to Holden, and we faced the officiant. Adrenaline surged through my system leaving me jittery and happy, and excited. My hands wouldn't stop shaking.

"We are gathered..." The officiant started talking and I couldn't hear anything but the sound of my own heartbeat pounding in my ears. Holden was next to me keeping my hands steady. I felt as if I would shiver apart into stardust and glitter.

"Makenzie," I stared into the officiant's eyes, and she had to repeat herself.

"Yes, of course," I said, forgetting everything from the rehearsal the night before. "Oh right, repeat after you."

I said the words. I knew my brother had handed me the ring, but at that moment it felt as if it had magically appeared in my palm. I slid the ring on Holden's finger. It was a chunk of gold, a solid gold band, sturdy and steadfast in its representation of our bond and commitment to each other.

Holden had to hold my hand still, as I continued to shake. The ring he slipped over my finger was a V-shape studded in garnet and amethyst representing our girls' birthdays in January and February. They were close together, but unlike my brother and me, they each had their own birthday.

I continued to stare at the ring on my finger, and Holden's thumb as he stroked it over my hand. The next thing I was aware of was Holden tipping my chin up so that he could kiss me.

We were married. After years of hiding and heartbreak, we were finally together. And married. Holden lifted Ainsley into his arms and the three of us walked up the aisle and out of the chapel.

I hadn't wanted a big ceremony, but both my mother and Holden's insisted on inviting everyone they knew. We compromised. The ceremony was smaller, while the reception took over the entire country club.

I smiled and thanked people I didn't even know. I lost track of who was supposed to be watching my girls, when I saw my mother without either of my children, I panicked.

"Sh, they are safe," Holden reassured me.

"But where are they?"

He leaned me to the side and pointed through a gap in the crowd. "They're over there."

He was right, they were as safe as they could be with their manny, Ethan. When it had been time for him to return to school in the fall Ainsley had been heartbroken. But after finishing his second year, Ethan returned to Nantucket and asked if he could have his old job back. I still hadn't found a nanny that fit our family as well as he had. With a new-born in arms and a rambunctious four-year-old, it was an offer I couldn't refuse.

"Come on, everyone wants us to dance so they can open the dance floor."

I let Holden lead me to the dance floor. I hung my arms around his neck and let him sway me to some song our mother's picked since they vetoed anything modern that we had wanted. It was fine, it wasn't as if we were going to do some fancy dance moves. Holden was still healing. He was still rebuilding strength in his limbs, but he no longer limped unless he was tired, and he never used a cane anymore.

The song changed, and I was spun off to dance with my father. Dancing with him was work. He insisted on dance moves that I had never learned. I barely knew how to waltz, forget about a foxtrot.

"Come on Mak, it's a basic two-step."

As if I knew what that meant. Holden was dancing with his mother. I knew there was a level of melancholy there without his father being able to see us get married or having ever known that he had a grandchild.

The music changed and I was dancing with Travis. "Save me from Dad. He's a terrible dancer."

I moved easily with my brother. He seemed to know what he was doing, and I felt as if I knew how to dance with him.

He and Holden had mended their friendship. We were still working on ours. He was actually a funny guy when he was trying to make me miserable. It turned out that Travis knew more than just how to dance. His financial investigation skills ended up saving Holden and his mother a lot of money, and any further embarrassment. Several offshore accounts in the islands were located, liquidated, and more properly invested.

He was the best man for a reason. He was still my brother, and we still had our issues. But I no longer hated him. He had even learned enough about the sewing craft industry to be helpful when it came to business decisions.

It felt like hours of smiling, cake, and toasts, so many toasts. Then came the speeches. Travis stood and made an opening fit for a stand-up comic, and then he did something that was worth his weight in gold.

"I'm here to say the things that people at weddings always think, but never say. No one wants to hear me embarrass my sister or my brother-in-law, least of all them. So, this is my speech, and the first of many gifts I hope to give you over the rest of our lives. No more speeches. I'm not even sorry if you prepared something. We are not drunk enough to care."

I applauded him enthusiastically. My mother ran out to the floor and grabbed the microphone away from him. She started to say something, but he made a 'cut it off' gesture with a finger across his neck and the microphone went dead.

"Travis, what have you done?'

"I've paid the sound guy a lot of money so we can enjoy this party, and not listen to a bunch of windbags talking. Any time someone picks up the mic, he will cut them off."

I kissed my brother on the cheek. "Thank you."

Holden joined us in the middle of the floor. He crushed me to his side and shook Travis's hand. He gazed down at me and kissed me. "Let's get out of here."

Before my mother could protest, Holden had me out the doors and into the back of a limo. When we got home— Ainsley and I moved in with him since we had only been staying in my parents' house— he swept me up into his arms and carried me across the threshold and into the house.

"Home," he sighed before putting me down.

"I've never been happier that you came home to me."

"I've always thought of this place as home, every summer here, with you. And now you are my home. Always."

When he kissed me this time, I knew what he meant. He would always be my home too.

The next book in this series, "**Doctor Daddy**" is now available. **Grab it HERE!**

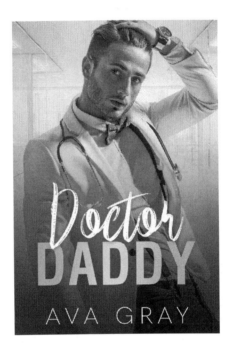

EXCERPT: BILLIONAIRE AND THE BARISTA

I should've known better...

Dating a bad boy biker could've only led to one thing: *Heartbreak.*

But that wasn't even the end of it.

The entire ordeal also gave me a baby.

One that I kept from him.

Before you judge me, know that he was the one to walk away and move to another country.

For years, I missed looking into Nathan's eyes.

I missed the way he would touch me.

The way he would speed up my heart rate.

So I wasn't surprised when I made the same mistake years later...

Another shot at love.... *And* another pregnancy.

I'm buried under all my secrets.

And history is likely to repeat itself... How will we both mess it up this time around?

Gabriella

Wind tore through my hair. I held tight to Nathan as he guided his Ducati Panigale in and out of traffic. He leaned and I let his body do all the work. I laughed as I tightened my arms around his muscled chest. I never felt freer, happier than when I was on the back of a bike with Nathan.

He drove too fast, he always did. I trusted him. He had eagle eyes and the reflexes of a cat. He took us far out of the city, deep into the country of Illinois, where we could ride with nothing getting in the way. Our helmets were clipped out of the way until we would need them again.

I didn't know where we were, didn't care. I was with him, and we were happy. Nathan slowed the bike and pulled to the side of the road. We were next to a field dotted with white and purple cover, and other wildflowers. After he helped me from the pillion seat I wandered into the field.

My fingers brushed some of the taller plants. I couldn't have stopped the smile on my face if I had wanted to. The sun felt good, on my skin. I loved the stillness of the air after the exhilarating rush of being on the bike. The contrasts were night and day, and just as beautiful in their own ways.

I spun for the sake of spinning. I didn't know if life could get any better than this. Especially with the way Nathan was looking at me.

"What?" I asked.

"What what, Gabby?"

He leaned against the bike. It was a sleek model, all fast lines and power with a custom black and red lightning paint job. The bike was as expensive and impressive as the man leaning against it. He was long-limbed and dangerous looking with his eyes hidden behind dark aviators. His thick dark hair was a shaggy mess from the wind. His smile flashed perfect teeth, movie star white and dazzling. His lips quirked into a sexy smirk, and the way he crossed his tanned arms emphasized the bulge of his muscles.

He was gorgeous, and he had spent the past six month looking at me like I was something beautiful and amazing. The way he looked at me stopped my breath in my throat and quickened my pulse. It was almost as thrilling as his kisses, and the way he touched me.

I skipped over to him and held out a few of the wildflowers I had picked. He took one of the lacey white flowers and tucked it into my hair, behind my ear. And then he leaned into me and kissed me. His lips were always a perfection on mine. Soft, warm, and he always used the right amount of pressing, the perfect play and tease. I tied my arms around his neck and tried to give him as good of a kiss as he gave me. Nathan's kisses curled my toes and tugged at things deep in my body every single time. I could let him kiss me forever and be content.

But kissing Nathan came with extras. He rarely just kissed me. He touched me, and his touch skyrocketed feelings and emotions straight into the stratosphere. My mouth may have been pleased with his expert kisses, but my body was not. I craved his skin against mine, his hands on me.

I leaned more into him and hiked my leg up against his hip. His hand ran over my thigh.

"Damn, woman, you are insatiable," he grumbled against my neck as his lips trailed kisses like fire down my neck.

"I've never done it outside, and there's nobody around."

Nathan pulled the skirt of my sundress up and slid his hand under my panties to cup me. He stroked a finger over my slit.

"You are wet," he chuckled.

"I've been on the back of a motorcycle, and you turn me on," I confessed.

He slid his finger in between my folds and circled my clit.

I gasped at his touch. It was everything I ever wanted. I may have been fantasizing about a quilted blanket out in the middle of the wildflowers, our bodies naked to the sun and the fresh air. Nathan above me, loving me, commanding my body. But I would take this. I would accept any touch he was willing to give.

He continued to kiss and run his lips over my shoulders before returning his mouth to mine. He tangled his hand deep into my hair while his other hand drove me wild with his touch. He teased me until

I couldn't focus. I scrambled for his fly, wanting to feel his hot cock in my hand. I wanted to give to him the way he was giving to me.

I managed to slip my hand through the open fly, and then I couldn't think. It was all I could do to hold on. His fingers were magic, and I was close to that edge he drove me to every time he made love to me. I moaned into his mouth as an orgasm crashed over me.

Nathan drove his fingers into me, and over my nerve center until I was putty in his hands, literally. He slid his fingers from me, and held me as I came down from the sudden high, he gave my body. He pulled my hand from his cock.

"But I want to make you feel good," I would have whined, if I had the energy. Nathan had reduced me to liquid, with no resistance.

"You do make me feel good, baby. You will later. I need to be able to focus. Wanting you gives me an edge," he growled, and pulled me hard against him. I didn't want this day to end.

He propped me back up on the pillion and climbed on. I had fantasies about Nathan, dreams of where and how I wanted his body, in a field, on his bike, on a balcony, in a pool. I wanted him always, even after he satisfied me on the side of the road, out in the middle of nowhere.

We rode for hours. It was dark by the time he pulled over and handed my helmet over before we crossed the border and returned to helmet laws.

The next time he pulled over we were in an upper-class neighborhood, in front of some mansion with a gated drive. There were dozens of other expensive racing bikes, as well as a collection of fast looking low sports cars. The people here had serious money. Nathan paused after I dismounted the bike. He ran his hands through my hair. It felt attentive and intimate, even though I knew he was fixing my helmet hair. He ran his hands through his own hair a few times. He took my hand and I followed him along a low-lit walkway.

The sounds of a DJ lured us to promises of a good time. We rounded a corner and the back pool area of someone's mansion was glowing with party lights, and pulsing dance music.

People laughed and splashed in the pool. Nathan smiled and waved at people he knew. Someone handed us drinks in red plastic cups. Nathan's friends did not run in the same circles that mine did. Before I met him, I had never simply walked into a party in the back of some mansion. With Nathan, we were in and out of pool houses, drinking champagne out of plastic cups, and dancing to touring DJs.

A girl I didn't know hugged Nathan and kissed him on the cheek. He spun her to the side. "Carmen, this is my Gabriella," he introduced me.

I wanted to burst the way he claimed me as his.

Carmen practically squealed and kissed me on both cheeks. She was glamourous and thin with perfect makeup and perfect accessories. I was completely envious of the easy manner in which she greeted Nathan and smiled at me as if she hadn't noticed me at first, but was delighted that I was there. "Gabriella, such a delight to meet you. Oh honey, you look like you got a little sunburn."

I glanced down at my arms. I was a little pink. "We were out riding," I said. "This will turn into a tan in a day."

I lied. I would stay pink, and then everything would freckle. I hated it. I wanted perfectly smooth tanned skin like the woman in front of me. I would be spotted at the end of the summer no matter how much sunscreen I slathered on.

Nathan kissed my shoulder, as if he knew what I was thinking. He gave me a wink, and I relaxed. I hated feeling awkward around his friends. And even though I knew he had done magical things to my body earlier, and would again before we parted ways for the night, I still couldn't help but be a little afraid he would change his mind and want to go home with one of the beautiful, polished women that were always at these parties.

Carmen left, and was replaced by another woman, equally perfect, kissing his cheeks, kissing mine. What was this lifestyle that I had no clue about?

I dragged Nathan into the area of the patio in front of the DJ booth. This was how I had seduced him the first time, this was where I knew he was mine, on the dance floor. With his hands on my hips, we moved back and forth, in the give and take that fit with the salsa style dance music the DJ played. I loved to dance, I loved to move. It must be why I loved being on the back of his bike as he raced through the streets.

As the night wore on, I found myself with my feet in the pool. I would have loved to go swimming, but I didn't have party appropriate swimwear. I didn't look like a model, and I suspected that was definitely a requirement to be allowed in a bathing suit at this party. Not that anyone said anything to me, and only a few people snuck sneaking glances at me. This was a party for the thin, rich, and beautiful. I was neither thin nor rich. But I had to think that I was beautiful because Nathan looked at me like I was. And his opinion was the only one that mattered to me.

Nathan handed me a drink in another red plastic cup. He sat next to me, keeping his legs away from the edge of the pool, and out of the water.

"You look pensive this evening. What are you thinking?" I loved how he wanted to know what I was thinking. It wasn't always about him.

"Stupid stuff," I said. I wasn't feeling as confident as I had earlier when he had been kissing me.

"I was thinking too, all day actually."

"Oh, yeah?"

"Yeah. I was thinking we should get married at some point. What do you think?"

My stomach clenched. I had to force myself to breathe and not jump up and down. His words were not what I had initially thought they might be.

"That wasn't a proposal, was it?" I laughed nervously.

"Not yet. Just thinking, we'd be good together. Don't you think so?"

We were good together. I thought it was an amazing idea. I wanted to say, 'I do.'

"Hmm, hmm," I hummed out a positive reaction while dampening down the excitement I felt. Nathan wanted to marry me.

Read the full story here!

SUBSCRIBE TO MY MAILING LIST

I hope you enjoyed reading this book.

In case you would like to receive information on my latest releases, price promotions, and any special giveaways, then I would recommend you to subscribe to my mailing list.

You can do so now by using the subscription link below.

SUBSCRIBE TO AVA GRAY's MAILING LIST!

Printed in Great Britain
by Amazon

29585481R00124